Dear Reader,

Welcome back to Lancaster, Maine! Get ready for another mystery with Jan and Elaine, along with delicious new tea blends and, of course, a mystery to solve.

If you're reading this, I have no doubt that you are a book lover just like I am. I've always enjoyed few things above curling up with a wonderful book and getting lost in the characters' world. But some books stay with us more permanently, don't they? For me, a lot of the books I read as a child have had a lasting impact on my life, and I've never forgotten those stories even as the years have gone on and I've filled up with plenty of new ones. There's just something about those childhood classics.

For Jan and Elaine, one of those favorite authors is the fictional Phillip Camden, and when the town of Lancaster is gifted with a relic of the famous author, the cousins are beyond thrilled! Until it goes missing...and Jan and Elaine are caught up in a web of literature and lies.

I had such great fun writing this new addition to the Tearoom Mysteries series, and I hope you'll have a wonderful time reading it. Without further ado, curl up with a cup of tea and enjoy!

Blessings,
Amy Woods

Tearoom Mysteries

TEAROOM *mysteries*

A Monumental Mystery

AMY WOODS

Guideposts
New York

Tearoom Mysteries is a trademark of Guideposts

Published by Guideposts Books & Inspirational Media
110 William Street
New York, New York 10038
Guideposts.org

Acknowledgments

Every attempt has been made to credit the sources of copyrighted material used in this book. If any such acknowledgment has been inadvertently omitted or miscredited, receipt of such information would be appreciated.

Scripture references are from the following sources: *The Holy Bible,* King James Version (KJV). *The Holy Bible, New International Version.* Copyright ©1973, 1978, 1984, 2011 by Biblica, Inc. Used by permission of Zondervan. All rights reserved worldwide. www.zondervan.com

Cover and interior design by Müllerhaus
Cover illustration by Ross Jones, represented by Deborah Wolfe, Ltd.
Typeset by Aptara, Inc.

Printed and bound in the United States of America
10 9 8 7 6 5 4 3 2 1

CHAPTER ONE

Elaine Cook stole a brief moment to step back and survey the morning's progress in the Lancaster Public Library, and smiled at the result. "It looks wonderful, doesn't it, Archie?" she asked, clasping her hands together, unable to contain her excitement.

"It does indeed," Archie Bentham answered, turning toward her. She and her cousin, Jan Blake, had hired the older British man some time ago as an employee at Tea for Two, the Victorian tea shop they owned and operated out of their shared home. "Everything looks just right—I'm certain Nathan will be pleased, and the board will be thrilled once they discover the big surprise." Archie's hazel eyes shone with satisfaction at a job well done.

Elaine nodded with shared enthusiasm and the two set off in separate directions to finish getting everything ready. She and Archie had left Tea for Two before dawn to decorate and prepare a library meeting room for what she hoped would be a very special day.

Her beau, Nathan Culver, an auctioneer, had been selected to appraise and locate a permanent place to display a recently rediscovered statue of the famous Maine author, Phillip Camden. She'd rarely seen Nathan so excited—being entrusted with a task of such magnitude had brought out the young man in the nearly sixty-year-old—and he seemed to have a little extra pep in his step these days. Antiques were more than just a career to Nathan—they were a passion—and the statue was by far the largest and most valuable piece he'd ever been hired to handle.

Elaine and Jan had been over the moon when he'd asked their growing tea and pastry business to cater the event, and the two women had spent weeks developing the perfect menu and curating decorations that would give the unique occasion the spark it deserved.

Dubbed by critics "the Charles Dickens of rural Maine," author Phillip Camden was considered a hero in the town of Lancaster, having grown up there and written and set most of his books locally and in surrounding areas. His stories had enchanted both children and adults for decades beyond his death in the early twentieth century, and all of his books were still in print and continued to grace best-seller and academic reading lists alike.

Elaine cherished many fond memories of her father reading Camden's stories to her at bedtime, a tradition she'd carried over to her own children when they were young. She still kept treasured copies of several of Camden's books, and even owned a first edition of her all-time favorite, *The Wind Speaks Softly*. The story held Camden's trademark blend of mystery and intrigue, hope and forgiveness, loss and love, faith and friendship. Elaine made a mental note to pull it out and read it again soon—what a wonderful way to spend a January afternoon, tucked under a blanket on the sofa in the upstairs sitting room with a steaming mug of tea.

Until recently, the location of the antique bronze likeness of Camden was unknown. It was only upon the death of its reclusive owner that the statue had been rediscovered, and the owner's will decreed that the sculpture be placed in Lancaster, the town he felt would most appreciate it and benefit from owning it. Since that time, it had rested safely in Nathan's care.

The unveiling party, on the other hand, was in Elaine's, and she couldn't wait for the library board to see what Nathan had in store for them this morning! Just as she'd been thinking of him, Nathan joined her at the long conference table, where she fussed with the garland surrounding the centerpiece she'd commissioned from a Portland artist—an ice sculpture of a single shelf holding gorgeously carved depictions of Phillip Camden's most famous works.

"That is truly a thing of beauty," Nathan complimented, placing a gentle hand on Elaine's shoulder as she nervously arranged and rearranged a single piece of dark-green foliage. "But it can't compete with my view," he said.

His words pulled her out of distraction and she turned to offer a smile at the sight of his tall, slim frame and light-brown hair, sprinkled here and there with little flecks of grey. He really was very handsome, she thought, feeling her cheeks grow warm as they always seemed to do when Nathan was around.

Friends since childhood because their fathers had been good pals, she and Nathan had officially been dating for several months now. Having lost her husband just over two years ago, she had found great comfort in Nathan's companionship in recent months, but it had taken the man no small effort to convince her that the two of them would make a wonderful couple. Of course, he'd been right, and now his presence never failed to brighten her day.

"Well, I'm so glad you like the decorations," she said, glossing over his flirtatious compliment. "I just hope the board feels the same."

Nathan's eyes softened and Elaine caught those dear little crinkles of age and laughter at the corners. "I have no doubt that they'll absolutely love it. Once again, you've outdone yourself, and Tea for Two can add another success to its growing repertoire."

"Now don't you speak too soon, Nathan," she chastised, shaking a finger. "The meeting hasn't even started yet."

He only winked before heading over to the podium at the front of the room to review his notes one last time. But, she had to admit, it was difficult to maintain modesty as she quickly checked her watch and took one final glance around the beautifully decorated room.

Earlier, when Nathan had told Elaine about the statue and his role as its caretaker, he had also informed her of his plan to surprise the board with such a gift. Keeping the secret from locals at the tearoom had taken some work. Phillip Camden's fame would make Lancaster the home of a great treasure, and it could even boost tourism for years to come. She couldn't wait until the whole town knew.

It was an honor to have a chance to take part in the secret statue's unveiling and, with hard work, she and Archie had transformed the ordinary conference room into a loving tribute to Camden's lifetime of writing. Framed prints of the Maine wilderness the author had loved so much adorned the walls, and streamers made from the pages of old recycled books hung from the ceiling. The large center table was lit by candles in antique brass holders, rendering the ordinary room a passage into Camden's Victorian-era America.

Jan had gone all out with the cooking and baking. There were little triangle-shaped cucumber and cream cheese sand-wiches, cupcakes adorned with tiny colorful stacks of fondant books, and black tea macarons with honey buttercream, just waiting to be savored. Elaine's cousin had labored for hours over those macarons, shooing anyone who dared interrupt her away from the kitchen until she'd finished meticulously piping rich buttercream between each fragile cookie. The impressive end result was definitely worth the effort.

And their other employee, Rose Young, had chosen a light, fruity herbal tea blend of lemongrass, rose hips, and pink pep-percorn that she'd named The Wind Speaks Soft-Tea, after the book of Camden's that Elaine loved so much, to accompany the culinary delights and to provide a break from the frigid winter air outside the library doors. Jan and Rose had stayed back at the tearoom to serve the bustling breakfast crowd that morning, but Elaine knew they would be just as proud of the outcome as she was.

On that note, she pulled her cell phone out of her apron pocket and took a few hurried snaps of the room, eager to show Jan and Rose the fruits of their labor when she returned to Tea for Two later that afternoon.

In moments, the library board—a fancy name, really, for the simple collection of townsfolk who helped Priscilla Gates, the librarian, oversee the care and function of the facility—would arrive, and the statue would be revealed. The board members had no idea what was coming their way, and already the room held an unmistakable sense of anticipation.

"All right then, it's just about time," Nathan said, eyes sparkling with unbridled eagerness. "All set?" he asked, glancing between Elaine and Archie.

The two nodded at each other and Archie said with an exaggerated flourish of his hand and a little bow, "Ready when you are. Go ahead and show them in."

Nathan nodded and sent an anxious look in Elaine's direction, his features presenting an odd mix of excitement and nerves. Her heart went out to him, and she said a silent little prayer that God would bless the statue unveiling and allow things to proceed without a hitch.

Positioning herself near the front so that she could welcome the board members and point them in the direction of refreshments, Elaine pulled in a deep breath. Soon enough, they began to file in, their faces pleasant but bemused—wondering, no doubt, what Nathan had in store for them.

The board consisted of six volunteers, most of whom either had a particular interest in books, were simply invested in the health and well-being of their local library, or, in a few cases, both. Katelyn Grande Conrad, the youngest and newest board member, was the first to walk into the meeting room, her pretty eyes lighting up behind dark-framed glasses as she absorbed the decorations.

"Wow!" she exclaimed, doing a little spin so as not to miss anything. "This is delightful."

Elaine beamed and ushered the young woman toward Archie, who held out a cup filled to its brim with steaming tea.

Bristol Payson, owner of the Bookworm bookstore, and Will Trexler, octogenarian inventor of a very effective—and very lucrative—insect repellant, and the library's most generous donor, followed. When Macy Atherton, owner of Green Glade Cottages and member of the Bookworm Book Club sauntered in, she crossed her arms and squinted at the decorations.

"Well," Macy said, her tone giving away the slightest hint of judgment and suspicion, "I don't know what on earth you've got planned here, but I hope the surprise doesn't give any of us a heart attack, if you know what I mean." Macy glanced briefly in Will's direction and winked.

Elaine caught herself just in time to prevent an audible gasp. "I'm sure that's not likely to happen," Elaine said, patting Macy on the arm as she directed her to the refreshments area, where Archie continued to serve up sizeable helpings of treats. "It should be a good surprise rather than a shocking one."

"I suppose we'll see soon enough," Macy said, heading off to the pastries with a huff.

As Elaine turned back to the door to welcome the last few folks, she indulged in a little pride on Nathan's behalf at the full turnout. Though there were only a handful of board members, she knew from chats with Priscilla that most meetings were missing a person or two, presumably because the older woman in charge of reading the minutes had a slight tendency to go on about them for longer than necessary. She was known for taking copious notes and, consequently, for reading through them meticulously and, well…slowly. As if on cue, that very person, Margaret Childers, entered and made a beeline for Jan's macarons, with a small wave to Elaine serving as her greeting. She was followed shortly by Priscilla.

"Well, hello there, Elaine," Priscilla said in her soft voice, offering a friendly smile. "How are you?"

Elaine took the librarian's hand and shook it gently. Initially, Jan and Priscilla had become good friends, and Elaine had wished for a stronger friendship with the librarian, but for some reason she hadn't taken to Elaine in quite the same way at first. But recently, she and Priscilla had been forging a wonderful friendship. "I'm just fine, and you?"

"Oh, I'm well enough." Priscilla looked around the room with large, curious eyes, tucking a strand of chocolate-brown hair behind one ear. "I just can't wait to find out what Nathan has up his sleeve. He talked to me about this surprise weeks ago and, after some coaxing, I agreed to let him keep it in the storage room. I know it's huge, but I can't for the life of me figure out what he's got hiding in there."

Elaine grinned. "Believe me, you won't be disappointed."

"In that case, I'm even more eager to know. I do enjoy a surprise now and then," Priscilla said, the slight rise in the pitch of her voice hinting at her exhilaration. Then she leaned in closer to Elaine and whispered, "Speaking of surprises, I see this meeting has greater than average attendance already."

The two women chuckled in unison.

"I guess all it takes to bring more folks out to our gatherings is a little mystery," Priscilla said.

"I'd say you're right on the nose." Elaine winked at the librarian and then pointed her in the direction of the table at which Archie was serving tea. Elaine was happy to see that, in addition to their teacups, almost everyone now carried a plate of goodies. After about twenty minutes, the visiting chatter began to quiet down, and the group gradually settled into their chairs at the long mahogany table.

Elaine and Archie quickly cleared snack debris away from the refreshments area and moved to stand at the back of the room, doing their best to be as quiet as church mice. Nathan caught Elaine's eye and she gave him a thumbs-up, hoping her encouragement would quell his nerves.

Priscilla officially called the board meeting to begin, Will seconded the motion, and after they took their seats, Nathan cleared his throat and welcomed the attendees. The board members focused their full attention toward his podium and Elaine was pleased to hear laughter as he made a little joke to set his listeners at ease. After a few introductory comments, he began to speak about Phillip Camden's influence on Lancaster and on the whole of literature—how the author's work was and continued to be a testament to the rugged and pure, but often harsh, beauty of outdoor Maine, and its parallels to the challenging ups and downs of life itself. Elaine felt herself drawn in by the descriptions of some of her favorite novels, their beloved characters, and the scenery each evoked, and when she looked around she could see that the board members were equally enthralled, waiting with bated breath to discover what Nathan's speech would lead up to.

"Finally," Nathan said, his eyes shining as he held on to the last few seconds of his secret, "we've come to the moment you've all been waiting for."

Even though Elaine already knew the secret, Nathan's contagious eagerness made her feel as though she were hearing it for the very first time. She looked over at Archie, whose right hand rested in a fist over his mouth, as though he couldn't wait any longer for Nathan to spill the beans.

"I recently received the great honor of managing the placement and future welfare of a very special gift, bestowed to the town of Lancaster by Jonathan Frost, a collector of antiques and a lover of the author about whom I've been speaking. Unfortunately, Mr. Frost is no longer with us. However, he has endowed this town with something very special from his private archive, something I think Lancaster residents and visitors will enjoy for years to come. This long-lost antique is bound to quickly become a treasure for our great town. Also, I would like to propose, if everyone is in agreement, of course, that the existence of it be kept mum, and that the board officially unveil the gift to the whole town at the upcoming annual library fund-raising event. Nothing has ever been more certain to bring in donations than what I'm about to present to you."

At that, Nathan called toward the back of the room, "Archie, if you would be so kind as to let Chris in."

Archie hurried to the entrance and pulled open the heavy wooden door, fastening it to its built-in stopper. As he stepped aside, Chris Cosgrove, a part-time work-study library assistant and also the quarterback of the Claremore Raiders football team, pushed a low, wheeled metal cart into the room. Atop the cart was a huge object—as tall as Chris himself and a few feet wide—hidden by a burgundy velvet coverlet. Chris stopped the cart close to Nathan's podium and stood back to wait for further instruction.

All eyes were glued to the form hidden underneath that cover.

"As many of you are aware, a well-known but not often seen commemorative work of art regarding Phillip Camden has been missing for decades. Sculpted by an obscure but talented artist and last spotted in the latter part of the twentieth century, that piece was assumed missing—or, worse, destroyed—until very recently. I am pleased to tell you today that this piece of art, thanks to Mr. Frost's estate, now belongs to the town of Lancaster, and I am certain it will be an absolutely wonderful decoration at the Lancaster Public Library's entrance, as well as a beloved attraction for locals and tourists alike, for generations."

When Nathan paused, Elaine saw several mouths open wide as the board members slowly began to realize what they were about to behold. The room was suddenly so silent that Elaine could hear the winter wind howling outside the thick library walls.

Nathan stood poised to reveal the gift, months' worth of pent-up energy threatening to burst out of him. Elaine could almost feel him buzzing with it, even from all the way across the room.

"Without further ado...," Nathan said, motioning for Chris to pull off the cover.

Chris complied, the young man's lanky arms reaching for the corners of the dark-red velvet. His motions were slow and

Elaine could sense the board members' growing anticipation. Even she, having heard Nathan talk about the piece but not actually laid eyes on it yet, could hardly stand to wait any longer.

Nathan reached out both arms as the coverlet rose up, up, up, and, finally, off the object it covered. "I give you the mysterious statue of the late, great author, Phillip Camden."

And in that moment, the previous silence disappeared, replaced by the collective intake of breath of every board member seated at the table, along with Elaine, Archie, Chris, and Nathan himself, as they all noticed the same unfortunate, terrible truth.

There was no statue to be found underneath that cover.

The stunned gasp quickly built to a loud rumble, questioning what on earth had happened and whether they were all the unfortunate witnesses of some sort of bizarre prank. Elaine gazed at what stood in place of the beautiful bronze statue they had all been expecting: an old clothing mannequin, dressed in a T-shirt, overalls, and a lumberjack hat.

Her body immobilized by shock, Elaine moved her eyes until they met Nathan's, which were full of despair, and she sensed him reach a conclusion at the same time she did—that the very valuable, very special statue of Phillip Camden...had been stolen.

CHAPTER TWO

Everyone in the meeting room stared at Nathan. Though in reality it was only a moment, it seemed like hours passed before anyone dared to speak. Finally, Elaine heard Priscilla clear her throat. "Nathan?" the librarian asked reluctantly, slowly standing up from her chair. "This may seem an obvious question, but do you have any idea what might have happened to the Camden statue?"

Nathan swallowed, his eyes huge as he stared at the mannequin. When he spoke, his usually strong voice came out no louder than a squeak. "No," was all he said.

Elaine's throat caught as she watched him struggle, unable to think of anything to say that might offer comfort.

Priscilla cleared her throat. "I suppose the next step then is to contact law enforcement and see if we can start the process of finding out what happened and where it is." Everyone else remained silent.

Nathan nodded too and his eyes began to clear, leaving space for his expression to change to irritation. "Forgive me for being at a loss for words—I just can't believe someone would do something like this."

"Excuse me," Macy piped up, standing, "but are we sure the statue was stolen? Maybe it's still just in the storage room and Chris grabbed the wrong item."

All eyes shifted to the young man and he began to shake his head. "Nope," Chris said. "When I went to the storage room to get it just now, like Mr. Culver and I talked about, the only thing in there—well, at least this size—was that." He pointed at the offending mannequin. "All that's in there besides that is a bunch of old books and files and stuff." He shrugged and scratched his head. "Now that I think about it, it felt much lighter than a big thing made of bronze."

His comment might have been funny if they hadn't all been so shocked and upset. Archie stood next to Elaine, rubbing his chin. When Elaine glanced at him, he raised both arms as if to say, "What in the world?" She bit her lip and made her way to Nathan's side. Words still eluded her, but if nothing else, she could show her support with proximity.

Nathan turned to face her, his skin pale and clammy, before he addressed the board again. "This is awful. I've had that statue waiting safely in the storage room for weeks."

"That's right," Priscilla added. "It was covered with that velvet blanket, so I didn't know what it was, but Nathan convinced me to let him and Mr. Frost's people store it here, though"— she went silent for a second and seemed to be rummaging through her memory—"I have to admit I haven't seen it since then. I rarely go into the storage room except once a year or so, when I do inventory."

"Then it must be theft," Will said, holding up his palms.

"Right," Elaine said, as several faces turned in her direction. "The question is, of course, who took the statue?"

"And why?" Priscilla asked. "Why would anyone do such a thing?"

"Exactly," Nathan jumped in, a little of his color having returned. Elaine thought he looked determined now. "Only Chris and I knew about the statue's presence here in the storage room. Though I'm sure other locals in the antiques business might have guessed." He looked down at his feet and Elaine patted his hand. "It was supposed to be a wonderful surprise."

"It certainly would have been," Katelyn said. "I still can't believe Mr. Frost decided to just give the statue to Lancaster—it's bound to be valuable."

Nathan said dejectedly, "Yes, it is that. From what his family has shared with me, Mr. Frost was very rich at one point, and enjoyed purchasing art and sculptures. Frost was a devoted fan of Phillip Camden and it's my understanding that he just wanted the piece to find a home in the place that so inspired the author. It wasn't ever meant to be sold." He wrung his hands together. "It was meant to be enjoyed by Camden's readers—all the people whose lives were touched by his books."

"It still will be," Bristol chimed in, as cheerily as any of them could manage.

Elaine nodded in agreement. "Yes, that's right. It still will be. We will find out who took the statue, and make sure it's returned to the place Frost wanted."

"It sure would have been nice to have that statue as the centerpiece of the fund-raiser," Margaret said sadly. "The last few years haven't been too successful." Katelyn placed a comforting hand on the older woman's shoulder, murmuring softly that things would work out in the end and that, somehow, the library would raise the extra money it needed for the following year's special programs.

"I suppose this isn't the best time to mention that I was counting on this surprise to draw a crowd at the fund-raiser. After Nathan told me how big it would be, I decided not to fuss with other attention-grabbers," Priscilla said.

A flush of red traveled up Nathan's neck and the librarian sent him a sympathetic look. "It's not your fault," she added.

"Regardless of who's responsible," Macy said, "we need to call the authorities and report this straight away."

Elaine was still reeling over the shock of what had happened, but Macy couldn't have been more correct. Whoever had stolen the statue of Phillip Camden could be on a path far, far away from the scene of the crime, and with the upcoming fund-raiser just over two weeks away, the clock had already begun to tick.

With Elaine standing by his side, Nathan put in the call. Dan Benson, a Maine state trooper who lived locally and was often the first responder in emergency situations, arrived about half an hour later. He apologized for the delay as Priscilla and Elaine met him at the front of the library and led him to the meeting room.

"I would have been here sooner but one of the little ones is sick and Charlotte is visiting her sister, so it's just me and the kids. Finding a sitter at the last minute was a little challenging." He took a knitted cap off his head and held it at his side.

She'd thought he looked a little strange and Elaine noticed then that he wasn't wearing his uniform but rather faded jeans and a casual heavy coat. She wished again that the statue hadn't gone missing and that Dan could be back at home, warm and cozy with his kids. For that matter, she wished that she too could be at home, happily helping Jan and Rose serve the regular morning customers, and that this whole thing was just a bad dream.

But perhaps that was a little selfish, she thought as she glanced at Nathan and saw the confusion, embarrassment, and sadness still lingering on his features. He needed her, and she vowed again to do everything she could to help him get that statue back.

"Couldn't the dispatcher have sent someone else?" Priscilla asked, concern causing her brow to furrow.

"Well, yes," Dan answered, "but—to tell you the truth—I could use a little break and a case to solve." He grinned sheepishly. "Those kids are my whole world, and I wouldn't trade them for anything, but after a week of singing along with their favorite CDs and watching the same movies over and over, I was happy to come along and investigate."

Recalling the days when her own children were small, Elaine couldn't help but smile at the trooper's contented but harried appearance. Thinking of Sasha and Jared gave her some perspective and helped to calm her nerves.

Archie offered Dan a cup of tea, which he politely declined, and as the board members milled about talking in soft whispers, Nathan relayed what they knew so far, which was, admittedly, not much at all. Dan began by talking with Nathan, but as the morning went on, each member added details that others had missed. Elaine only wished the actual crime had so many witnesses.

After talking with the group for some time, Dan retrieved a kit from his vehicle and spent a little while dusting for prints in the meeting room and on the library doors and windows. Eventually the board members dissipated, excusing themselves to previous engagements, each promising to get in contact with the trooper if they thought of anything that might help. Priscilla had closed the library for the meeting that morning, but Chris said he had some shelving to catch up on and headed to the stacks, leaving Priscilla, Archie, Elaine, and Nathan alone with the trooper.

Dan flipped his notebook shut. "I'd like to see the storage room now, if that's all right with you."

"Of course," Nathan said, leading the way, his shoulders sagging with palpable disappointment and, Elaine suspected, many other emotions. As soon as she had an opportunity, she would ask if he'd like to come back to the tearoom for a respite from everything that had happened, and for a chance to chat with her. She hoped that together they might be able to toss ideas back and forth about who would be inclined to commit such a strange crime. Unfortunately, knowing how few people were even aware that the statue still existed, it would be a very short list.

The light was still on in the storage room from when Chris had retrieved what was supposed to be the statue. Aside from the mannequin that Chris had wheeled back into storage once they'd called law enforcement, the young man had been correct—a quick look around revealed only a slew of file boxes and several shelves of old, dusty books. Dan set to work again, quickly dusting the room and the mannequin for prints.

"Not much to see, is there?" Dan asked, tucking what he'd obtained into an evidence bag and packing up his kit. "There's nothing valuable in here that would have lured a criminal, that's for sure."

"That means the culprit must have known the statue was in here," Elaine pointed out. "I think we can assume it wasn't just random."

"Right, but only Frost's executor, the movers he hired to bring the statue here, Chris, and I knew its whereabouts," Nathan added, having explained earlier to Dan how the statue came to be in his possession. "Jan, Elaine, and Archie didn't know where I stored it, but they were aware of the statue because I asked them to help with today's meeting. As far as I know, that's everyone. And when I checked on it yesterday before lunch, the statue was in place under the cover, ready for today. Archie, Elaine, and I were here early this morning to set up, but I didn't think to look in on it again."

Dan's mouth formed a thin line. "Okay, since you saw the statue yesterday before noon, and you, Archie, and Elaine were here early this morning, that means our window could be anywhere from yesterday afternoon, to any time during last night. And, Priscilla, I assume you would have mentioned if you had, but just to clarify—you didn't by any chance see anyone towing the statue out of the library before closing up yesterday?"

She chuckled until she saw that Dan was serious. "No."

Dan jotted a few notes, then looked up. "Won't do much good to stress about it. We'll do the best we can to find out who did this, and hopefully we can get it back to you before the fund-raiser."

The fund-raiser was now on everyone's mind. As a member of the Lancaster community, Dan would want the sculpture returned as much as any other citizen.

"Unfortunately, though, since you were the last to see it, Nathan, I do need to ask you a couple of routine questions," he added.

Elaine saw Nathan swallow, and she squeezed his upper arm. It was just a formality. Surely Dan didn't suspect Nathan had made arrangements to relocate and hide the statue for himself.

"Ask away," Nathan said, pulling his shoulders up.

Dan nodded and checked his notepad. "Do you mind telling me where you were last night? And this morning?"

Elaine was surprised when Nathan's body tensed beside her, but she supposed anyone would be nervous, being questioned by an officer of the law.

"I was, um, at home," Nathan said slowly, as if tracing back through his steps. "And then here, preparing for this presentation," he added.

Elaine's heart lurched as she thought back to the night before. She had actually called Nathan's house around nine thirty and there was no answer. Slightly worried at the late hour but thinking perhaps he'd just gone out to grab a few items from the store or was in the shower or something, she'd texted him as well, but hadn't gotten any answer until around ten fifteen. At that point, he'd simply responded by saying good night and that he was off to bed.

Dan asked a couple more questions and then closed his notebook, standing up. "That's it for now," he said, giving Nathan a sympathetic look. "If I need anything else, I'll give you a call."

Nathan nodded distractedly.

"Now, Priscilla," Dan said. "Same question for you..."

Priscilla showed a time-stamped picture of her out to dinner with some friends the night before, followed by a parking app she had on her phone which showed when and where she parked. "I use this app because I have been known to lose track of where I park at places like SuperMart, but you can see it shows I parked at home last night after dinner and then again this morning at the library."

Though Elaine was listening to Priscilla's answer, she was distracted by Nathan. Something was off. She saw him release a long breath when Dan looked away.

After Dan and Priscilla finished that conversation, he moved through the room thoughtfully. He examined the mannequin. "So what can you tell me about this mannequin, Nathan?"

Nathan was fidgeting with a pen in his hand and didn't seem to hear Dan.

"Nathan?"

"Yes? Oh, I'm sorry. I just can't believe that this has happened. What was your question?"

Dan asked Nathan the question again. "Well, it's definitely an antique," Nathan answered. "And unique. Likely from the early 1900s, made of plaster and wood. And *very* valuable." The emphasis on the word *very* was lost on no one.

Dan nodded, writing down the new information. Nathan pinched the bridge of his nose, then grabbed his cell phone from his pocket and flipped his thumb over the screen. He sighed before looking up again and showed Dan the phone. "Here's a photo of what the statue looked like; I'll email it to you. I'd already consulted with several experts and we were in the process of coming up with an exact figure. You see, Mr. Frost—the collector who willed it to Lancaster whom I spoke of earlier—wanted the statue to remain here in town. It wasn't intended to be sold at all."

"The person or people who took it must have somehow deduced its value," Dan muttered, mostly to himself, as he continued to scribble in his pad. "So, this is no ordinary theft. We're looking for a criminal with knowledge of Phillip Camden or the statue—probably both. Someone who would know its history and value."

Nathan cleared a table of some books, sending a heap of dust billowing into the air, then helped the trooper lift the mannequin and lay it on the surface, supine. They examined it in silence, until Elaine heard Dan say "Huh" from where he stood near its plaster feet.

"What is it?" Nathan asked.

Dan bent over and squinted at something. "Looks like some kind of marking." He straightened his back. "Come on over here," he said, waving a hand. "Have any of you seen anything like this before?"

Elaine stepped nearer and peered at the mark Dan pointed to on the mannequin's left heel. Up close, she recognized the tiny label, a logo formed with the letters H and E. "I do recognize it," she said, glad she finally had something useful to offer. "It's the label Harrison Ellerby uses to mark items in his store. I've seen it before while researching a mystery for Macy."

Dan made a note but didn't seem overly intrigued. "I'll drop by and talk to Harrison—maybe he knows where this guy came from," he said, pointing a thumb at the mannequin. "In the meantime, I think I'll head back to my office and get started on an official report and make some phone calls to nearby pawn and antique shops. If something this large was stolen, it would stick out like a sore thumb. I don't think anyone would be that bold, but you never know. I'll also call some of my law enforcement contacts and let them know to look out for it, especially at the docks where it could get shipped off before we have a chance to find it."

He turned to Nathan. "At your earliest convenience, I'd like for you to draw up a list of independent antique dealers in the area so we can check with them."

Nathan, Priscilla, and Elaine nodded solemnly, and Dan offered a smile that was obviously meant to be encouraging. "We'll all work together to figure out where that statue went and we'll get it back, okay?"

The four of them left the storage room and Nathan, looking pale, excused himself to the men's room, mumbling something about a quick stop to splash his face with cold water. As Nathan walked toward the restroom, Dan asked Priscilla to keep the library closed and locked until he could return in the morning to finish up and collect surveillance tapes.

As they exited the room and headed toward Priscilla's office, Dan asked her who'd had access to the storage room.

Priscilla sighed deeply. "No one could have gotten into the storage room except Nathan and me. We're the only two people who have a key."

Dan pursed his lips. "And there's no sign of forced entry. Still, it's possible that someone hid in the library before you closed up last night, and took it after you left."

"I would never have thought so," Priscilla said, her skin going pale as she considered the idea of someone lurking around without her knowledge, "but I guess it's possible." Chris Cosgrove had been waiting near the door. Dan beckoned him in, and he came over to join the conversation.

"You've got that right," Dan went on. "This early on in an investigation, I find it helps to keep an open mind."

Suddenly, a funny look crossed Priscilla's features. "There is something else," she said.

"What's that?" Dan asked.

"I'm sure it doesn't mean anything…" Priscilla responded sheepishly, glancing around.

Elaine listened carefully as Priscilla continued, eager for another clue or piece of evidence.

"I tried calling Nathan twice last night, just to confirm what time he would be here this morning. Both times, there was no answer, and he didn't call me back."

Elaine felt her stomach drop as she matched up Priscilla's timeline to her own, in which she hadn't heard from Nathan until ten fifteen the night before. Still, she was certain it was nothing that couldn't be explained.

Just then, Chris chimed in. "It's funny," he said. "I don't think this means anything either, but I saw Mr. Culver going into Ellerby's antique shop the other day."

Dan shrugged his shoulders. "That makes sense. Nathan specializes in antiques. I would be surprised if those two *didn't* consult on pieces pretty often."

"Yeah, I know," Chris said. He didn't look convinced. "The thing is, Mr. Culver looked...different than usual."

"What do you mean?" Dan scrunched his forehead.

"It's just that he was wearing weird clothes. I mean, not weird necessarily—just that they weren't like what he usually wears, you know, work clothes. The other day, he was wearing a black hoodie sweatshirt and black pants."

"Huh," Dan said noncommittally while jotting something down.

Elaine watched as the trooper closed his notebook. "You know," he said, "I've read before about that statue being presumed lost forever and I never thought anything of it. I used to read Camden stories as a young boy, and I guess I just can't believe we're now dealing with a real-life mystery surrounding that relic. It's almost like something out of one of his old books, isn't it?"

Elaine nodded, hoping life would imitate art and that, as in Camden's books, everything would turn out okay in the end.

NATHAN, BACK FROM the men's room, left to walk Dan out to the trooper's vehicle and then to help Archie load the refreshment supplies into Elaine's car. Alone for a moment back in the meeting room as she boxed up leftover pastries, Elaine sighed heavily as the weight of the last few hours' events pressed down on her shoulders.

Surely Nathan, the man she'd come to love, couldn't be guilty of a crime? He wouldn't steal the Phillip Camden statue. He had no reason to do so. Yet a little part of her asked, *Did he? Could he?*

Yes, Nathan was an experienced antiques dealer and yes, he was aware of the value such a piece could demand, but that was precisely it—he was successful at his job, widely trusted in his field, so there was no reason for him to do such a thing. He wouldn't risk his reputation and the extensive client list he'd worked so hard to build over the years. And besides, the look on his face and the pride in his voice when he'd announced the arrival of the statue to the library board spoke volumes. He wanted the Camden sculpture to belong to the town more than anyone. He'd been looking forward to the fund-raiser with elation.

Elaine shook her head, and with a tug at her heart, realized she was missing the point entirely. Instantly, she put a stop to the line of thinking she'd allowed herself to follow thus far.

Motive didn't matter at all because of one simple truth: she trusted Nathan. That was all there was to it. She didn't need any proof to know deep down that he wasn't to blame for the statue's disappearance.

Unfortunately, law enforcement wouldn't see it the same way—they would need proof that someone else committed the crime. As of yet, they couldn't prove that Nathan did in fact steal the statue, but Elaine had seen the suspicion in Dan's eyes, and soon, if they couldn't prove he didn't do it, she'd see it in the eyes of everyone in town. Her belief in Nathan's innocence wasn't enough to clear him of theft. That would take basic hard detective work, and she was up to the job.

Elaine steeled herself against the knowledge of what was ahead. She could do this. She and Jan had solved several mysteries since moving to Lancaster and opening Tea for Two, and this one would be no different.

With that, she determined to put her anxious energy to better use. Heading down the hall toward the storage room, she grabbed the fingerprint kit she kept in her purse nowadays.

Once in the small room, she opened the kit and examined the items inside: a pair of gloves, a magnetic applicator and small jar of black magnetic powder, a roll of tape, and a set of small white cardboard squares on which to save any prints she managed to lift.

Finally alone with the mannequin, she would have to work quickly because Nathan would come looking for her soon, and she did not want to have to explain where she had been.

From the box, Elaine selected the gloves and drew them on, then picked out the applicator and powder. "Now where would I place my hands if I were going to pick you up?" she asked the inanimate figure. "Ah, here I think." She recalled Dan dusting the same area. After examining the form as best she could in the dim light, she took off the mannequin's shirt and set it aside. Most mannequins were sold without clothing, so whoever decided to switch it out for the statue probably did so after dressing it.

Next, Elaine removed the cap from her kit's magnetic powder and dipped in the little brush, shaking off the surplus before slowly swiping it over the areas just underneath the mannequin's armpits, where she thought it would be easiest for a person to lift.

The mannequin was made of plaster and wood, which were problematic in and of themselves because of their porousness. However, the torso, head, hands, and feet were coated with a thick-looking layer of paint, and that would be much easier to work with. She allowed herself a little grin when an array of swirly marks appeared, but it didn't take long for that grin to be replaced with a frown. Trying a selection of other spots on the mannequin didn't seem to help. Only a few partial prints had emerged in the powder, and she knew from experience that those probably wouldn't help. Though she'd had success with the fingerprint kit before, it seemed this time would be different.

At any rate, she tore off a piece of cellophane tape and pressed it down on the most complete portion of print she'd found, allowing the powder to stick to it before transferring it to one of the white cards and placing it into a baggie. She did the same for the other partials and then quickly shoved everything back in her purse, just in time to hear the door creak open.

"Elaine?" Archie asked, brows lifted in question when he met her eyes. "What are you doing in here? Is everything all right?"

"Yes, I'm fine. I just wanted to get another look at this mannequin before we head back to the tea shop."

"Ah, I see," he said, eyeing the discarded shirt, still lying on a nearby table. "Another one of your mysteries."

Elaine carefully replaced the article of clothing, and then Archie motioned for her to come along and join him. "I've cleared away all the refreshments," he said. "Let's get back to the shop, shall we? I think it's been a long enough day already and we both deserve a hot cup of tea and a cookie."

Elaine picked up her purse and headed through the door that he held open for her. "I think that sounds like a good plan," she answered, willing her voice to project less worry than she truly felt.

For the first time, Elaine found herself hoping that the fingerprints she'd lifted wouldn't be solid enough to point to anything, because, no matter how hard she tried to convince herself otherwise, a tiny part of her still worried that she—or, worse, Trooper Benson's team—might find a match to Nathan's.

CHAPTER THREE

That same morning, Jan had hurried between tables at Tea for Two, doing her best to keep up with the early crowd of locals and a handful of visiting faces she didn't recognize. She was very glad Rose was scheduled to work alongside her that day because they were exceptionally busy and Elaine and Archie had gone to cater the special library board meeting for a few hours.

Thinking of her cousin and Archie, and hoping the pastries she'd baked were a hit, Jan glanced at the chiming antique clock on the wall on her way to refill the teapot she was carrying. *Wonder what's keeping those two?* she thought, making a mental note to check with Rose the next time she and the young woman ended up in the kitchen at the same time. Archie and Elaine should have been back by now.

Meanwhile, Jan refocused her attention on keeping the customers happy. Her best guess was that the bitter-cold January air and another round of snow had driven many Lancaster residents out of their homes in search of hot drinks and pastries to warm their bellies, and good conversation to warm their souls.

With the Maine weather as it was, and with everything back in business this side of Christmas, Jan knew it could certainly get lonely staying indoors for too long, especially for people who lived by themselves. And with that thought, she found herself giving silent thanks for what must have been the hundredth time that she didn't have to live alone.

Since she and her cousin had opened the tearoom coming up on two years ago, her life had been delightfully full of people. With her husband having passed over a decade before, she'd even begun dating a wonderful man named Bob—a lawyer and childhood friend of Elaine's—though the thought of him saddened her now. Bob had gone to Baltimore the previous fall to pursue an exciting job opportunity, and even though they Skyped regularly, Jan had to admit she missed him a lot. She usually looked forward to chatting with him, but lately, with them both so busy and with so many miles between them, Jan had begun to wonder if they could really make it work. It was hard to imagine a future with Bob so far away, and because his plans to stay in Baltimore were indefinite, Jan didn't know if she could hang on to a long-distance relationship forever. Even though it was painful to think about, she'd begun to wonder—could it be time to let go?

Still, she had so much to be thankful for, including the beautiful Victorian home she and Elaine had turned into a successful business.

Even now, she couldn't quite believe she got to live and work in such a place. The house, built in the early 1900s, was set on the shore of Chickadee Lake, and boasted white walls with three types of decorative wooden shingles, several gables, and even a tower that reminded Jan of something from the pages of a fairy tale. The main floor had a spacious entry and two parlors, one on either side, which she and Elaine had transformed into old-fashioned tearooms. The second floor hosted several large bedrooms, one of each belonging to Jan and Elaine, and one of which they'd turned into a sitting room for just the two of them to enjoy. And in the summer, she loved to sit on the home's wraparound porch and work on puzzles from her favorite magazine, *Cryptograms*. But the house carried its own winter beauty as well, the heavy snow making it look like something that Thomas Kinkade might have painted.

She absolutely loved living and working there, even on busy days like today.

In the kitchen, she filled a teapot with a fresh brew of plum ginger tea, a warm, wintery blend of sweet plum, cranberry, fig, orange peels, cinnamon, and of course ginger. The smell caused Jan to close her eyes so she could savor it as it wafted into the air. Everyone loved the new flavor so far, and she couldn't wait to offer it throughout the rest of January.

With a full pot in hand and a tray of piping-hot mini maple croissants and plum tarts straight out of the oven, she headed back into the fray. She stopped at a table in the west parlor occupied by two newcomers she didn't recognize. To Jan, the two young men appeared to be about college-aged, and they were wearing the same blue T-shirt with a moving company logo on the front.

"Good morning and welcome to Tea for Two," she began brightly, and they both went on to order the plum ginger tea and four of the plum tarts from her tray. One of the guys was very polite and seemed to want to chat, telling Jan that the tearoom reminded him so much of his grandmother's Victorian home that he just had to stop in following a big moving job the night before. The other wasn't quite as friendly and didn't say much to Jan, but as she was serving their tea and pastries, she overheard him telling the outgoing one that the two really did not have time to stop for breakfast.

He kept looking nervously at his watch, making a big show of checking the time. "We really should get going," he said, seeming to ignore Jan. "I don't feel too good about that last-minute job from last night, even though the money was too good to turn down. Plus, we've still got a load to drop off at the docks, and then we've got to hightail it back to Augusta if we're gonna make it on time to the last job of the day."

"Well, I'm so glad you came in," Jan said, smiling at both of them, hoping her cheer would rub off on the not-so-friendly one. She hoped their day would go well. "Please let me know if there's anything else I can get you." Just then, she remembered the jar on a table in the entry hall. "Make sure you drop a business card in the jar on your way out!" she called, heading off to help another table. "We're drawing for a giveaway of a dozen pastries!"

She wondered about the job they'd been discussing, musing briefly that it was a little odd for a small moving company (at least she didn't recognize the name as a chain) from Augusta to assign work in Lancaster, but then again maybe it was someone moving to a new house or something. At any rate, the thought slipped easily from her mind when someone nearby began to call her name.

Jan turned to see Clifton Young seating himself at a corner table. She smiled and carried her teapot and tray over to the spot he'd chosen. "Hi there, Clifton," she said. "How are you this morning?"

Clifton was Rose's father and becoming something of a regular, following his wife's death a year and a half prior. He'd especially been coming in a lot over the past month or so, Jan noticed. Jan's heart softened each time she saw him, familiar as she was with the loss of a spouse. Her own husband had passed a very long time ago, but the pain never completely went away, and she could still recall what it was like when it had been new.

"Better, now that you're here," Clifton answered, clearing away space for Jan to set her tray and teapot.

Clifton's face visibly brightened at the sight of her and Jan had a passing thought to suggest to Rose that her father might want to get out more. She knew Clifton was an orthodontist and a selectman, and that he shared an older Cape Cod family home in Lancaster with Rose, but she didn't know if he engaged in any activities purely for the social aspect. A recent memory of Rose mentioning that her dad didn't take his motorboat out as much as he used to popped into Jan's mind, and she decided to spare a few minutes to chat with him. A quick glance around reassured her that Rose had everything under control, at least for the moment.

"Business looks good," he continued.

Feeling a little guilty at doing so, Jan sat down, promising herself she'd only stay a moment and would get up instantly if

Rose seemed the least bit overwhelmed. "Yes, we're thankful it is," she said. "With this weather, you never know. Most old Mainers like myself will take any chance they can to get out of the house when it's this cold, but lots of folks newer to the area would rather do just about anything but."

Clifton laughed and Jan noticed again how white his mustache and beard were for a man of his age. They made him look distinguished. "Well, I can only speak for myself, but there's no place I'd rather be on a cold morning. You and Elaine have the best tea selection I've ever seen, and I've enjoyed everything I've tried." He grinned. "Now that's saying something for a guy who prefers coffee."

Jan couldn't help but warm at the compliment. "Thank you so much," she said. "We do our best to offer interesting choices, and I have to say, I never would have thought it could be so much fun to flip through a tea catalog every season and pick out anything I'd like. We really enjoy coming up with our own specialty blends too."

"It is a uniquely excellent feeling to find success at a job you enjoy," Clifton said.

"I couldn't agree more." Jan motioned to the teapot and Clifton nodded, turning over the upside-down cup on the saucer in front of him. "Speaking of—how is your practice going?"

"Oh, you know, the usual—braces and such. I'm fortunate that teeth don't often arrange themselves in nice, neat rows, so things stay fairly busy."

He gave her a shy smile and then looked down into his empty teacup, his very bald head catching a glint of sunlight from a nearby window.

She filled his cup. "I think you'll like this blend. It's fast becoming a favorite and in my opinion it's the perfect mix of sweet and spicy." Settling back in her chair, Jan watched as Clifton took a sip.

"Ah, you're right. It's delicious." He set down the cup. "Do you mind?" he asked, reaching for a plum tart.

"Not at all," Jan said, shaking her head. "They wouldn't be very useful if they weren't for eating, now would they?"

Clifton grinned and took a big bite, closing his eyes. "I don't know which is better: the tea or the pastry."

Jan felt a surge of pride—she loved to bake and continued to become more adventurous in the treats she made for the shop. "Fortunately, you don't have to choose."

Clifton finished another tart and a croissant and, though she enjoyed the small talk, Jan began to get the feeling that Mr. Young had something he wanted to ask her, or was it something he wanted to share with her? She couldn't put her finger on it, but after a few moments, unable to think of a polite way to ask him if something was on his mind, Jan became restless and eager to get back to work. Plus, she hadn't seen Rose come back out of the kitchen and she needed to get in there and check on the batch of lemon scones she just remembered she'd left in the oven.

"I've had a great time talking to you, Clifton," she said, trying to be gentle while also conveying the sense that she needed to serve other customers. "Would you like me to let Rose know you're here so she can come and say hello?"

Jan didn't have a chance to hear his answer because, at that moment, Archie burst into the front hall, followed shortly by

Elaine. The two appeared in the parlor doorway, waving at Jan as unobtrusively as they could, obviously agitated by something.

Jan turned to Clifton and excused herself, wondering what could possibly have happened at a Lancaster Public Library board meeting to cause the two to appear so disturbed. If she hadn't known better, she might have thought Clifton looked a touch too unhappy to see her go, but she was sure she had it wrong. She chalked it up to the loneliness that inevitably follows the loss of a loved one, and went on her way, thinking she would mention his visit to Rose and ask if everything was all right with the young woman's father.

When she reached the parlor doorway, Archie was kind enough to take the tray and teapot from her, and the three made their way back to the kitchen. In the split second she'd caught sight of her cousin's face, Jan had noticed Elaine's eyes were wide as saucers.

"What's gotten into you two?" she asked when she was sure that none of the customers could hear.

Elaine and Archie looked at each other, their expressions a disconcerting mix of distress and weariness. "You won't believe us when we tell you," Archie said, shaking his head.

CHAPTER FOUR

A rchie wasn't exaggerating when he said I wouldn't believe what happened at the library board meeting. I can hardly imagine that someone would steal that statue," Jan said later that evening. "Who would do such a thing to Nathan? He's one of the friendliest folks I know, and his business thrives on a reputation of integrity, so I can't believe that he's made enemies." Jan's brows knit and behind her glasses, there was concern in her blue eyes. Elaine could hear her own tension reflected in her cousin's voice.

Elaine stared at the window of their private upstairs sitting room as the winter evening darkened. She gripped her teacup tighter, aware that the bracing warm liquid within wouldn't help, but seeking comfort in it all the same. "It's beyond me," she said softly, feeling suddenly exhausted.

She wasn't really in the mood to talk about the statue anymore—what she craved now was a good night's sleep so she could wake up the next day ready to get to work and help catch the thief—but she understood that the day's events were new to Jan, and sharing the details with her cousin could only help.

As the old saying went, two heads were better than one. She and Jan had solved several local mysteries together, and Elaine held on to hope that this time things would turn out all right in the end, as they always had before.

"More importantly," Elaine continued, "Nathan was so looking forward to this event, but only a few people—including you and me—were aware that the statue exists, and not a one of us would want to sabotage him in such a way. If it's someone who wasn't in that boardroom today, then I'm at a loss about who it could be, and if it's someone who *was*—well, that would be even worse. These are our neighbors, people we know and trust."

Jan nodded with obvious sympathy. Elaine could feel her cousin studying her carefully as she spoke, and she could practically predict the question before Jan put it into words.

"I know it's been a pretty tough day for you. How are you holding up with all of this?" Jan asked, her expression full of warmth and concern.

Elaine glanced into her tea, sorting through a commotion of feelings. When she and Archie had returned to Tea for Two that afternoon and rehashed the details of the statue theft to catch up Jan and Rose, the parlor had still been full of customers, so there was not time to stop and think over what little evidence she had, and of course they had spent a while unloading supplies from the car and then washing and putting everything away. In a way, though, Elaine had welcomed the distraction. Now, however, as night drew near, she was certain sleep would elude her with all the details of the day rushing through her mind.

"To be honest, not so well. This wasn't an ordinary antique deal for Nathan—this event was the highlight of his year, possibly even his career. That it could be destroyed by theft never crossed my mind. And with the library fund-raiser coming up so soon, there is a lot riding on that statue."

Jan placed her teacup on an end table and reached over to settle a hand on Elaine's forearm for comfort. "This is serious, for sure, but nothing has been destroyed yet. There's still time to figure out what happened and to retrieve that statue. I know you're not willing to give up yet, and I'm here to help. We'll figure this out together, okay?" Jan patted her arm and then picked her cup back up and took a long sip. "Tomorrow. For now, you need to get some sleep."

Elaine nodded, sadly. She so badly wanted her cousin's words to be true, and in the morning, she would make a plan and set to work to get to the bottom of this. But at the back of her mind, the nagging worry would simply not let go.

THE NEXT MORNING, Elaine rose early and dressed quickly in a thick purple sweater and soft gray slacks before heading down to make a cup of espresso. The day ahead called for more fortification than tea could offer.

She had just finished adding a touch of sugar to the strong coffee when she heard Jan's footsteps on the old wooden stairs. A moment later her cousin joined Elaine in the kitchen, stretching her arms above her head.

"Did you manage to get any sleep?" Jan asked.

Elaine noticed Jan's eyes looked a little puffy—much like her own had when she'd been standing in front of the mirror to comb her hair. She wondered if maybe there was something bothering Jan and she made a mental note to ask about it later, rather than allowing her own preoccupation with the missing statue to keep her from being a good friend.

Elaine held up her espresso cup in lieu of a response, and Jan grinned, which made her look much more awake.

"I guess not," Jan said.

Elaine took a sip of the bracing liquid. "Both Rose and Archie are scheduled to work this afternoon?" she asked.

Jan nodded, turning on the stovetop to heat a kettle. "Yep to both. There's a good chance a storm will blow in after lunchtime, so we may have a slow spell later in the day with folks trying to make it home before the worst of it."

"That's good to hear," Elaine answered, following Jan over to the large pantry. "If things are calm, I'm going to make a quick trip to Waterville."

Jan glanced around for a few seconds, a finger resting on her bottom lip until her eyes settled on a container. "Ah, this should do for a day like today," she said, pulling out a plain satchel of English breakfast tea. "Practical and strong."

Elaine smiled. "Depends on how you define strong."

"Well, it certainly won't send me blasting off like a rocket the way that stuff you insist on drinking will"—she feigned a scoff at Elaine's dark, rich coffee—"but it will do just fine for me."

"If you say so," Elaine teased back. Even a little humor was a welcome relief after a night of tossing and turning, filled with fitful dreams. What she needed was to get out and do something to help, and at the moment, she only had one idea of where to start. It would just have to be sufficient for now.

"So, what's going on in Waterville?" Jan asked, pulling a teacup out of the cabinet, into which she placed the bag of English breakfast.

Elaine took a last sip of espresso and went to the sink to rinse out her cup. "Well, I'd like to stop in at Harrison Ellerby's shop and ask him some questions."

Jan's eyes widened but she didn't say anything. She didn't need to. A while back, Jan and Elaine helped solve a mystery in which the prickly antique store owner was a person of interest.

"Is he back at work after that theft incident?" Jan asked, raising an eyebrow. The kettle began to squeal and she grabbed a potholder before lifting it from the stove. She shut the burner off and poured boiling water over the tea bag.

Elaine finished rinsing her cup and placed it in the dishwasher. "I believe so. He was a suspect, as you recall, but ultimately, he was not charged with anything."

Jan crossed her arms and leaned against the counter, glancing at her watch.

Soon, Elaine knew, her cousin would begin baking something that would fill the tearoom with a delicious aroma, and in a few hours the first customers of the day would arrive. Likewise, Elaine would soon do a run-through of the parlor to make sure everything was clean and tidy, start the large kettle boiling, and check out front to see if any snow needed clearing. But for now, it was just the two of them, cherishing the quiet of the early part of the day. Since they'd begun sharing a home, their morning moments together had become a ritual she knew they both enjoyed.

"Still, I think it would be best if someone went along with you," Jan continued. "I'm sure Ellerby's none too happy to have you visiting again since the last time you encountered him, he ended up in hot water." She held up her steaming mug as she removed the teabag.

Elaine grinned. "Thanks, but that's not necessary. I'll be just fine going alone, and it will only take a little while. I'll be back before you know it to finish up with the afternoon customers and then you can take a long, well-deserved break while I close up for the day."

Elaine thought for sure her cousin would like the sound of that, especially after baking so many treats for the board meeting the day before, but for some reason, Jan was wearing a slight frown.

"What's the matter?"

"Oh, nothing," Jan said with a wave of her hand. "It's just that, well, I may have wanted to come along."

Elaine looked at her cousin in surprise and a little burst of laughter broke out. "You're too curious to stay here and let me go to Waterville on my own."

"I'm just looking out for my favorite cousin," Jan said, taking a sip of her tea, her blue eyes sparkling with mischief over the top of the mug.

Elaine rolled her eyes, pretending to be irritated. "Well, okay, you can join me. But if it's busy, neither one of us is going to Waterville."

"It's a deal," Jan agreed. "Now, before I let you off the hook, you've got to tell me what exactly you're going to ask him when we get there."

"I'll explain in the car," Elaine said, unable to help a giggle when Jan groaned in protest at having to wait.

It was not long after Jan had pulled a couple of trays of puffy, cream-filled danishes from the oven that the two women heard the front door swing open, and the day's work began. They spent the next several hours serving a busy morning crowd—mostly regular customers, but a few new faces as well. Not many people toured Maine in the winter, but every once in a while, a few brave tourists passed through.

In her time working at the tearoom, Elaine had met more than one visitor from the south who'd never seen snow and craved a real winter experience. And of course, business travelers sometimes stopped by on their way to one of the nearby cities. She'd even been surprised by the number of foreigners who'd visited them. It was one of the things she loved best about her new life—she never knew what kinds of people the day would bring, and each fresh greeting reminded her of God's wonderful creativity.

It was a good thing to think about as she put on a smile and tried hard not to worry too much about Nathan. He'd texted her that morning to ask how she was doing and her heart had gone soft, knowing that he was thinking of her when it was he who had so much to be troubled about. God had truly gifted her with a good man, and she felt doubly blessed to have loved twice in her life. It was difficult to be apart when such an awful thing was going on, but they both had busy lives to lead, and the moment she had a chance, she would see him again.

A little after lunchtime, things in the tearoom started to slow down, and when the last customer said goodbye and a half hour passed with no new visitors, Jan suggested they try to make it to Waterville before it started to snow. Archie and Rose had already arrived and were busily making the tables in both parlors ready for any new customers who might stop in. Wiping her hands on her apron, Elaine glanced out the front window at the view of Main Street. A few locals hurried past with shopping bags, but for the most part, the street was clear under a gray sky filled with low, heavy clouds. It would definitely snow, but there wasn't yet any sign of weather that would make driving to Waterville unsafe.

"Do you think it's a good idea to go out with a storm coming?" Elaine asked anyway, just to be cautious. She trusted Jan's judgment better than her own when it came to the weather since Jan had lived in central Maine all her life, whereas Elaine had spent thirty years moving all over the world with her late lieutenant-colonel husband.

Jan peered out the window, her eyes narrowed behind her glasses. "We've got a few hours at least before anything hits, and I don't think the bulk of it will fall until nighttime," she said with confidence.

"You're the boss," Elaine said. If Jan said it was okay, Elaine knew it likely would be. Her cousin was rarely wrong about the weather.

"I prefer 'resident meteorology expert,' if it's all the same to you," Jan teased.

Elaine gave a playful bow before heading to the kitchen to take off her apron and wash her hands. "I'll drive."

With that decided, the two women said goodbye to their employees, grabbed heavy coats, wrapped thick scarves around their necks, and pulled on gloves. Elaine kept a few water bottles and protein bars in the trunk of her car, along with thick blankets, just in case she ever got stranded, but as they headed outside, the sky appeared to have cleared a little, and she decided not to give it too much more thought. The road looked good as she backed her bright-red Chevy Malibu out of the garage, and she felt her shoulders begin to relax. Just the idea of doing something to help Nathan made her feel the slightest bit better.

Remembering her earlier promise to herself to ask what might be bugging her cousin, Elaine turned briefly to Jan, who stared pensively out the window at the passing asphalt.

"You've been good about making sure I'm okay with the statue missing, and I'm grateful—I truly am—but I couldn't help but notice earlier that something seems to be eating *you*."

Jan turned from the window and met Elaine's gaze before Elaine focused her eyes back on the road ahead.

"Oh, it's nothing," Jan said, suddenly shy.

"I know it's not nothing," Elaine gently prodded. "You've been staring off into the distance while you mix batter and when we got a chance to grab a quick lunch break today, I noticed you almost put sugar on your leftover pasta instead of salt."

Jan looked over, her mouth wide open. "I didn't know you saw that," she said.

"*Mmm-hmm.* I sure did." Elaine gave a chuckle but then her voice was more serious. "Don't worry—I promise I'm not trying to hover like I have in the past. I know you're strong. But I also know that you've been missing Bob badly since he headed back to Baltimore after Christmas. Is that what's bothering you?"

Elaine knew Jan missed him very much, but perhaps it had gotten more difficult in recent months to be apart from him. She would certainly miss Nathan if he moved so far away.

Jan bit her lower lip, thinking. "It is, and it isn't."

Elaine stayed silent as she drove on, knowing that sometimes keeping quiet was the best way to encourage someone to open up.

"Something interesting happened yesterday," Jan said. She seemed to be processing her own thoughts as she spoke. "Clifton Young came by the tearoom and I wasn't too busy, so I sat with him a spell."

"Rose's father is a good man," Elaine said.

"Yes," Jan said. "He was here for just a few moments—we chatted about his work and mine, but I also got the sense he may have wanted to speak to me about something more specific."

"What do you mean?" Elaine asked.

"Well, I can't put my finger on it really, but he seemed… more interested in me than I'd ever noticed before. He didn't ask after Rose or anything." Jan paused. "I had the feeling that if you and Archie hadn't come in when you did, he may have asked me to lunch or something." Jan shook her head as if not knowing quite what to make of it.

Elaine was starting to put the puzzle together in her mind, but she didn't want to put words into Jan's mouth. "Do you think that, possibly, he might have wanted it to be a… date?"

Jan looked over, her expression surprised, as if she hadn't expected Elaine to guess what she'd been uncertain about.

"Yes, that's exactly it." She looked down at her hands, the gloves off now that the car had warmed up. "But he didn't say anything that would make that clear, so I don't want to jump to conclusions."

"I see," Elaine said, going over this new information. "That's interesting. I guess I hadn't thought that he might be ready to have a new relationship, but come to think of it, it has been quite some time since Rose's mother passed."

"That's true, and we all grieve in different ways and on different timelines, but I suppose I hadn't given any thought to the idea before. I certainly hadn't noticed him giving me any more attention than any other person, but now that I look back on it, he always stops to chat with me a little more than with Archie or you."

Elaine could see that Jan was still sorting out her feelings on the subject, so she didn't want to show much of a reaction in case her cousin wasn't feeling welcoming toward Clifton's attention. He was a handsome, kind man with a great career, and he was a good father to Rose, but Elaine knew that Jan's attachment to Bob was strong, despite Bob's moving away from her and leaving their growing relationship on a sort of pause. Bob had come to visit and he and Jan video chatted pretty often, but lately, Jan seemed to feel a little down after their chats, rather than cheerful.

"How do you feel about the idea of going on a date with Clifton?" Elaine asked.

Jan tilted her head. "He hasn't asked, so thankfully I don't have to give it too much consideration, but I guess it might not be a bad thing to spend some time with him, as friends, and see what that's like."

Elaine felt her heart give a little tug. While her cousin was wonderful with the tearoom customers, Jan's personality was generally shyer and more reserved than her own. Regardless of what came of Clifton's potential interest, it was nice to see her putting herself out there.

"That sounds like a good way of looking at it," Elaine agreed.

"You don't think it's disloyal to Bob?"

"Having a friendly lunch with Clifton?" Elaine shook her head. "No, I don't think it's disloyal."

Jan nodded. "In that case—I think if he does ask me to lunch, I'll say yes."

Elaine smiled, hoping her words of encouragement helped. Regardless of what came of it, having a little friendly attention from another good guy might give Jan a break from wondering if she and Bob would ever be together permanently.

With that settled, Jan seemed to feel a little better. "Now, before we get there, I've got to know—what do you think Harrison Ellerby has to do with the missing Camden statue?"

Eyes still on the road, out of her peripheral vision Elaine saw Jan glancing around as they pulled into Waterville. She spotted Harrison's little shop in an old building that looked like any other in the small town. The only thing to distinguish it was large gold letters that spelled out the word *Antiques* above the door.

"Remember that mannequin I told you about? The one we found under the cover in place of the statue?" Elaine asked as she pulled into a parking spot near the middle of the city block.

Jan nodded.

"It had Ellerby's stamp on it. So, whether the man knows it or not, something, and possibly someone, from inside his store, was involved in taking that statue."

CHAPTER FIVE

This place looks perpetually gloomy," Jan said as she grabbed her purse and shut the passenger door of Elaine's Chevy.

"You're right," Elaine said. "Sometimes a place does reflect its owner," she added with a chuckle.

Elaine glanced up at the building as the two women strolled across the street. It looked even older than it had the last time she'd been there with Nathan, but there, on either side of the door like two eyes staring out into the street, were the same windows bordered by dark-brown wood. The storefront held the same sense of dark mystery she recalled from her former visit, and sparked a memory of something Nathan had mentioned—a warning of sorts that Harrison could be a prickly fellow. She grinned to herself. As if she could forget such a distinct personality.

"You could look around, like you're shopping for something in particular, while I see if I can find an assistant to talk to. I'd really prefer not to get Harrison involved too much—the more suspicious he is about our intention for being here, the more he'll shut down."

"Right," said Jan. "You know, I have been looking for an antique lace runner for the top of my bedroom bureau—perhaps he'd be able to help me out with that."

"Good thinking," Elaine agreed as she pulled open the door.

There was no pleasant tinkle of bells like one often found in small-town high-street shops, but walking into the store was like entering the estate sale of a very eccentric individual. Not unpleasant clutter, was the best way she could think to describe it.

Jan's eyes traveled eagerly over the haphazard arrangement of rare objects and with a little nod, she set off in the direction of a cabinet whose drawers were open and spilling out a mass of antique linens, leaving Elaine to examine the abundance of unique pieces near the door while she kept an eye out for Harrison himself.

The owner was nowhere to be seen, but after just a moment, a young man approached from behind the counter. His smile was genuine, but if she wasn't mistaken, there was an air of nervousness about him, as though he was in a hurry to manage her and then go back to whatever had occupied him before their entrance.

"Hello there," he said. "My name's Steve—I'm a new assistant here."

"Hi, Steve," Elaine responded. "It's nice to meet you. I'm Elaine and the woman I came in with is my cousin, Jan." She held out a hand, and one of Steve's shot out from his side to grasp hers and let it go in the quickest greeting she'd ever experienced. Its awkwardness almost made her laugh, and added to her curiosity over what was causing him to be so jittery.

"Is there something I can do for you?" he asked, gripping his thumbs and forefingers together in front of his apron. He had disheveled sandy-brown hair that flopped over one grayish-green eye like a small boy's might do, and he shook his head to move it aside.

"At the moment, I'm just browsing," Elaine said, "but I'll be sure to let you know if I don't find what I'm looking for."

Steve nodded rapidly, then turned as if to leave, before Elaine began to speak.

"Do you mind my asking if Harrison Ellerby is around?"

Yes, the young man was definitely nervous about something, she decided, because the color drained from his cheeks at the mention of his boss's name.

"Uh, yes, he's, uh, he's in the back working on a restoration project," Steve said before swallowing hard. "I'd be glad to get him for you if you like."

Elaine thought the tone of Steve's voice indicated he'd much prefer to do just about anything else, but all the same, he had offered. She gave him a warm smile, in the hope it would settle his nerves a little. She was dying to ask what was bothering him but had no reason to do so without seeming nosy.

"No, that's okay," she said instead.

Steve's relief was evident. "Okay then, I'll just be right over there if you need anything." He pointed to a workbench not too far from the counter.

She watched him turn to leave and focused her attention on the interior of the shop. The overhead lighting was dull, making the large room feel appropriately like an attic in which a person might find all the stuff that typically filled one. There was a tall chest of drawers with three antique suitcases staggered precariously on top, and large glass display cases holding various sets of vintage china. She tried not to get distracted by a shelf of antique teapots that caught her eye, but it was too late for Jan, who had begun to wander in that direction just as Elaine started to look away.

Surrounded by antiques, Elaine's thoughts turned to Nathan, and she sent him a quick text just to see if he was doing okay considering everything going on. Then she pretended to shop around for a bit until she spotted a group of mannequins near a corner toward the back of the store. As she neared them, she noticed that most of them were not very old at all—in fact they resembled the new, plastic sort found in a modern department store. It seemed that, rather than being displayed as items in their own right, their purpose was to model the vintage clothing they wore. She'd been hoping to find some similar to the one that had been discovered in the Camden statue's place. If Harrison wasn't in the habit of carrying antique mannequins, then why had the one they'd found had a sticker from his store on its foot?

Maybe there had been an older one in stock before. Or, it was certainly possible that it had been purchased elsewhere and a label stolen from Harrison's store had been added to throw off an investigation, but that seemed pretty unlikely. And anyway, who would think to go to such effort? It would have to be someone who knew Harrison's store, had access to the inside of it, and who'd be able to grab a sticker without being noticed.

Her mind wandered back to Steve, who was obviously the replacement for George Newsome, Harrison's former assistant. If Steve worked in the store regularly, taking one of his boss's trademark stickers wouldn't be difficult at all, and if Harrison had selected him to be more than just a cashier, then perhaps he had knowledge of antiques himself...maybe even enough to know the odd history of the Camden statue.

It wasn't much, but it was the only lead she had so far.

She turned to look for the young man at the workbench but he'd disappeared and, when she surveyed the entire room, was nowhere to be seen. However, when her gaze returned to the counter, she caught sight of Harrison striding out from the back area toward her, looking none too pleased to see her.

"Ms. Cook," he said, reluctantly reaching out a hand. "So nice to see you again."

There was unmistakable oiliness coating his words as he stared at Elaine with piercing eyes that reminded her of a vulture or some other predatory bird. He was obviously anxious to find out what she was doing in his store after her involvement in a mystery surrounding a stolen vase belonging to Macy Atherton. He'd been cleared later, but that obviously didn't mean he was willing to let bygones be bygones.

"It's nice to see you too, Harrison," she said, taking his very cold, thin hand. His presence was as foreboding as she remembered, and much of it had to do with his tall, thin, crane-like frame. His dark hair was combed to one side and slicked back, and he wore round glasses. Every piece of his clothing was completely black.

She could tell he was waiting for her to speak.

"What brings you in?" he asked, his words slow and calculated. "Are you here to shop this time, or for another reason?" He peered at her over the top of his glasses frames, and she told herself not to allow him to intimidate her.

Easier said than done.

"Jan and I"—she pointed a thumb in the direction of her cousin, who smiled and waved at Harrison—"were in the area and thought we'd stop by. Jan is interested in a lace runner for her dresser."

One of his eyebrows tweaked upward. "You couldn't find antique lace in Lancaster? Depending on the type you're looking for, old linen is not exactly rare. Value is derived from scarcity, attractiveness, the item's condition, and whether or not there is a demand, which I can assure you there is not currently for antique lace. Unless a piece of linen hails from royalty or some other special circumstance, it is unlikely to be valuable. Hence, Ms. Cook, I'm sure your cousin could have located a sufficient piece in your own...little town."

Wow, Elaine thought but somehow refrained from saying out loud. That was quite a lecture. Still, he was on to the fact that she wasn't really there to shop, and there wasn't much chance of evading his negative attention any longer.

"While we're here—," she began.

"Ah, so there is another reason you stopped by. I hope it's not to do with that unpleasant business with George. As you can see, I've hired a replacement. Though I still can't believe the audacity..." Harrison had a faraway look as he glanced over Elaine's shoulder.

She shook her head, hoping to reassure him. "It's nothing to do with that," she said. "All the same, I hope you're fully recovered from the incident, and I'm glad to see you back to work. I know there are not many who have your specific set of knowledge and skills, and it would be a shame for the antique world if you were not here."

She'd learned from Nathan that flattering Harrison Ellerby could go a long way toward getting the man to open up.

"While you're not wrong about my expertise, I must admit I'm eager to hear why you're really here. Please, do share," he said, crossing his thin arms over his angular torso. "Contrary to what you might believe, I do in fact have things to do outside the realm of fending off false accusations against me."

Elaine looked down. She was sorry about the situation, though a man who had a reputation for sometimes working with shady goods dealers shouldn't exactly be surprised to find himself in the middle of an investigation involving a missing antique. But it wouldn't do any good to say so—on the contrary, it would just ensure that Harrison would refuse to help, and she needed information that he might have.

"I don't know if you've caught wind of it yet, but something has happened to an object that was in Nathan's care."

One of Harrison's eyebrows shot up in curiosity. Elaine wasn't thrilled at the idea of telling him about the Camden statue's disappearance, but letting him in on it might persuade him to tell her if he knew anything. Besides, she thought with an internal groan, the whole town was going to find out before long, if they hadn't already. And, because of the stamp she'd found on the mannequin, she was almost certain Harrison himself didn't have anything to do with the theft. Surely he wouldn't have left his calling card if he'd stolen the statue.

"I can't say I have," he responded. "Though I did see Culver in here recently." There was a sinister gleam in Harrison's gaze. "He was wearing a black sweat suit, of all things, and asked about selling some items," Ellerby added, seeming to intentionally leave out what those items were, as if he hoped to provoke her into asking. "It wouldn't be very professional of me to talk about it further, however, as I take the privacy of my contacts very seriously." The shop owner held up his nails and inspected them, while keeping watch on Elaine out of the corner of his eye.

Your *shady* contacts, Elaine thought, before realizing the implication that her own Nathan could be one of them. She knew Ellerby had meant to agitate her, and she had to admit— he'd done a good job. She was dying to know what Nathan had been doing in the store, and why he hadn't mentioned a recent visit. But she would have to deal with that later. Right now, she needed to concentrate on the issue of the mannequin.

Figuring the best place to start was at the beginning, she relayed what she knew so far, and was not surprised to see the shop owner's eyes light up when she spoke of the statue.

"That is quite intriguing," he said. "Of course, I did know something of the statue's history, but I was not aware that it had been owned by a private collector who recently passed away." Harrison rubbed his sharp chin. "I don't have enough information to make an accurate estimate, but an educated guess would put its value well into the low six-figures."

Elaine studied Harrison as he spoke, but his expression indicated only genuine curiosity and interest. She didn't get the impression that he'd been involved in the theft. That did not mean, however, that his shop assistant was innocent. At that moment, Elaine turned her head slightly and saw Steve chatting with Jan out of the corner of her eye. Jan's introverted, calm nature seemed to make Steve more comfortable than Elaine had, and she hoped Jan, who was very observant, might notice any details about his behavior that she herself had missed.

"Yes, it is very valuable," Elaine said, nodding. "That's only one reason why the fact that it's missing is such a disaster."

"That's all very interesting," Harrison said, "but where do I come in?" He flashed a sinister, knowing grin. "You aren't under the impression that I had something to do with the theft, are you? Not *again?*"

Elaine was surprised to hear her earlier thoughts echoed out loud. "No, of course not," she said, hoping her voice sounded firm. "But I do think you might be able to help."

"And how is that?" he asked, sounding a little relieved despite his attempt to maintain the upper hand.

"Nathan intended to present the statue to the board, and instead, when the coverlet was removed, there was a mannequin in its place."

"So?"

"Not just any mannequin," Elaine added. "An antique one."

"And you want to know if I'm the one who sold the mannequin to your thief," Harrison said. "*Hmm,* I'm not in the habit of stocking those on a regular basis, but I do come across one on occasion."

Elaine nodded, hopeful, and described the mannequin to him. "It had one of your stickers on it—the same found on all of your merchandise." She described the logo.

"I can confirm that the clothing you've described the mannequin wearing is definitely not from my store. However, coincidentally perhaps, I do have a small supply of mannequins that was given to me recently after a store closed down. Steve was charged with the task of unloading them from the delivery truck and cleaning them for possible display—he's completed only two so far, and I haven't yet decided what to do with the rest." He waved a hand dismissively. "But, come to think of it, I do recall selling one the other day. It was the same day we got the shipment in that Steve was working on. I recall a fellow coming in and specifically asking for one, so we pulled one quickly from the new lot."

Elaine waited for him to ask if she'd like for him to check his records, but his silence indicated he wanted her to be the one making the request.

"If it's not too much trouble, I'd be grateful if you could check and see if the one sold sounds like the one we found."

Harrison seemed a little too pleased to hear her needing something from him, but she supposed that was fair, considering what he'd been through.

"I'll see what I can do," he said. "Let me go back into my office and check receipts from the last few weeks."

"Thanks so much. I'd really appreciate it," Elaine said.

He turned to go and Elaine glanced around, looking for Jan. Her heart sped up a little when she realized her cousin was nowhere in sight, so she headed for the door behind the counter, thinking maybe Jan had followed Steve to the back area in search of a runner like she'd mentioned. Glad it was unlocked, she pushed open the door, and gave a little sigh of relief when she saw Jan chatting with Steve.

"Ah, there you are," she said. "I've been looking for you."

Jan smiled "Steve here was just showing me this beautiful collection they recently received from an estate sale's leftovers." She held up a piece of delicate-looking eyelet lace.

"Harrison says it's not valuable," Steve added, "but I'd have to check on the price as it's not yet been added to our inventory."

"That would be lovely," Jan said.

"Before you do that, though," Elaine said, holding up a hand, "would you mind if I asked you something?"

Steve swallowed visibly. "Sure."

"It's just—are you feeling okay? I noticed earlier that you looked a little unwell."

A bead of perspiration formed near the young man's brow and Elaine felt a pang of sympathy for him. He looked as though his gears were spinning, possibly trying to decide what to tell them, but then, in a sudden burst, he told them everything he knew.

"I had a feeling you might be here for more than just antiques. Mr. Ellerby's talked about you being nos—I-I mean—*curious* about mysteries in the area. I didn't mean for it to happen," he said. "But last week, I was unloading a delivery from out back and putting the Ellerby labels on the items, the same lot that had your lace runner in it. And I came inside here for a minute—it was only a minute, because I'd heard the phone ring, but whoever it was hung up by the time I answered—and when I got back, I noticed that one of the old mannequins from the delivery was gone. Just like that." He snapped his fingers. "Somebody must have driven up and just taken it from the truck while I wasn't looking." He hung his head. "I did the research like Mr. Ellerby's taught me to, and found out the price."

Steve looked suddenly very guilty as he wiped moisture from his forehead.

"It's okay, Steve," Jan said softly, patting his arm. "It's not your fault that somebody took something."

His frown deepened. "That's just it, though. It *is* my fault since I shouldn't have left merchandise out there. It's just that Harrison was helping a guy up front—with another mannequin, come to think of it, and I was here by myself with a whole lot of work to do. It was quiet in the shop, so I thought I'd catch up on that new inventory, but I shouldn't have left it alone out back."

"It sounds like you were just a little overwhelmed," Elaine said. "It could have happened to anybody put in that position."

Steve nodded, looking a little better. "I was feeling pretty bad about it, though, so I paid for the thing myself, and if Harrison asks about it, I just planned to tell him that someone bought it."

Jan grinned. "That's true, though, isn't it?"

"I guess it is," Steve said before releasing a heavy breath.

"You did the right thing by paying for it," Elaine added. "If I might ask, though, do you happen to recall what the stolen mannequin looked like? And did you get a look at the person who took it?"

Steve shook his head, looking disappointed. "Well, I had only started unloading and we hadn't had a chance to appraise it yet, so I don't remember the exact details, but I do know it was old. It didn't look like any mannequin you'd find at a modern department store. And I didn't see the person who took it, but I think they might have been driving a truck, because I heard a pretty loud engine when I was coming back out of the store."

"Okay," Elaine said. "That helps." She was just about to ask if her cousin was ready to head on home, when Steve's head perked up.

"Wait!" he said, his forefinger shooting up into the air. "There was something weird about it—weird and kind of funny."

Elaine's heart beat faster. "What's that?"

Steve gave a little grin. "It was wearing a strange hat—a kind of plaid-looking thing."

The words bounced around inside her mind, as she tried to quickly work out why they sounded so familiar.

"Oh!" she exclaimed finally. "Like a lumberjack hat?"

Jan glanced between them, befuddled.

"Yes," Steve confirmed, "exactly like a lumberjack would wear."

Or, Elaine thought, like the mannequin in place of the statue had been wearing. Possibly—the *stolen* mannequin. She was excited to finally have a lead.

Harrison came back a moment later, holding a receipt and appearing slightly disappointed. Jan and Elaine looked at him expectantly.

"Well?" Elaine asked, unable to hide her impatience.

"It's not going to help you much. I did find the receipt and the mannequin I sold does not match the one you described."

Elaine and Jan glanced at each other and feigned disappointment, as they already knew where the lumberjack mannequin had come from.

"We're sorry to hear that," Jan said.

"Oh," Harrison said, "and I recall the customer saying that he needed it for an old wedding gown."

Elaine and Jan both nodded and thanked Harrison and Steve. Jan gathered up the lace runner, and the cousins headed to the car. They were glad to have had a positive encounter with Harrison—if that's what you could call it—and perhaps everything that had happened before regarding the missing antique from Green Glade was water under the bridge.

"So, the mannequin the thief put in place of the statue isn't the one that Harrison sold—it was the one stolen from out back when Steve was unloading the truck," Elaine said, thinking out loud in case she'd missed something.

"Right," Jan said. "It would have been so much more helpful if the one Harrison sold had been the one the thief put in place of the statue."

"Yes, it would," Elaine agreed. "Then we'd just have to persuade Harrison to show us that receipt."

"It is odd, though, don't you think, that the thief took a mannequin from Steve on the same day that Harrison sold one?" Jan pointed out.

"Yes, it is odd," Elaine answered. "Now we know for sure there's a thief, with two recent criminal acts, no less—the mannequin *and* the statue—but we're nowhere closer to catching him."

CHAPTER SIX

Jan's kitchen was awash with the marvelous scents of orange, clove, and pecan when Rose arrived the next morning to begin her shift. Jan was hard at work on a new muffin recipe that she anticipated would perk up the customers. A Mainer her whole life, Jan felt burnt out by the winter this year, and even though summer was still many months away, it might make things brighter if she could bring a little citrus fruit into their lives by combining it with the traditional winter flavor of clove. She'd splurged on a bag of oranges a few days before and couldn't wait to try it out.

"I know I say this nearly every day, but it smells incredible in here," Rose said, closing her eyes just after stepping through the kitchen door, having shed her heavy outerwear in the hallway. "Is that new?" she asked.

"*Mmm-hmm,*" Jan said, careful not to look up from the sharp microplane as she zested her fourth orange. "I'll let you be the guinea pig when I'm done with this first batch."

Just then Elaine came in through the back door that opened onto a screened porch. "Good morning," she said to Rose.

"Good morning to you," Rose answered. "How's that cat of yours?"

Elaine grinned. "You know Earl Grey. He's not really *our* cat."

Rose laughed, but Elaine was right—in a manner of speaking. Earl Grey was a stray cat who had wandered up in search of a home shortly after she and Jan had moved into the house. Since then, he'd become sort of half domesticated, but the stray in him was still dominant, and he was in the habit of coming and going as he pleased. For the most part, he spent his nights here, even when the temperature outside was cold. Elaine had constructed a warm little shelter for him after contacting an organization that worked with outdoor cats. The spoiled boy was also the proud owner of a heated water bowl, daily feedings, and a litter box on the porch.

"Footloose and fancy free," Rose quipped, winking at Jan over Elaine's shoulder. "A feline could certainly do worse."

Jan had to giggle at that little slice of truth.

"Anyway," Elaine said, the corners of her mouth also turned up in a slight smile, "he's doing just fine. I think he spent the night out there."

"It was a cold one," Jan said. "But thankfully the storm wasn't near as bad as anticipated."

"I didn't have too much trouble getting in today," Rose agreed.

"Cup of tea, Rose?" Jan heard Elaine offer.

Jan knew her cousin had been up early and already tidied and readied both parlors for the day. After their trip to Waterville the day before, Elaine seemed to be doing a little better— at least she had almost certainly confirmed that the mannequin that had replaced the Camden statue had been stolen from Harrison Ellerby's antique store—but as they'd driven home, Elaine had expressed frustration over still not having a solid lead. Jan wished she knew of something that would cheer her cousin up, something besides an orange muffin.

Rose asked for cinnamon apple tea. "That sounds good," Jan chimed in. "I'll have a cup as well."

"I was just about to ask," Elaine said, smiling.

Jan stopped zesting to glance up at the wall clock. "Rose, would you mind turning on the TV? That show I like is coming on. Channel twelve, I believe."

"Sure thing," Rose said, grabbing the nearby remote to switch on the small television Jan had recently placed in the kitchen to give her something to listen to during the many hours she spent baking.

Rose turned it to the correct channel and the first few strings of the introduction jingle for *Treasure Travels* poured out of the speakers. "Oh, I like this show too," Elaine said, filling a kettle with water. "I love when a guest is about to get rid of a bunch of old junk, and they find out that it's incredibly valuable."

"Me too," Jan agreed. "Last week, this woman found an old oil portrait while cleaning out her late mother's attic. She didn't think anything of it, but it turned out to be a member of a royal British family from the sixteenth century—worth a small fortune!"

"Sounds like fun," Rose said, glancing toward the television as she pulled three cups down from a cabinet and placed a cinnamon apple tea bag in each.

Elaine finished filling the kettle and turned on the burner, then went to the pantry for sugar and stopped by the fridge for milk. "I've only been watching it for a little while now, but apparently it's been on for years."

"I've never seen an episode," Rose said, "but I've heard that the two guys who host it are going through more than just a little drama these days."

Jan's ears pricked up. "They're brothers—Gary and Stuart Henderson." She finished zesting the last orange and headed to the sink to wash her hands and the microplane. "I'm not surprised to hear about the strife. Like so many siblings, they don't always see eye to eye, and it's definitely come up in an episode or two before."

"I'm sure the producers aren't in a rush to cut out any of that," Elaine added. "The more drama, it seems nowadays, the more viewers."

"You're right about that," Jan added, rinsing her hands and drying them off on a towel near the sink. "I guess in some TV, that makes sense, but it's a bit much on a little antiques program like *Treasure Travels*. I'm just in it for the interesting finds. I could do without the extra theatrics."

Elaine nodded just as the teakettle began to announce shrilly that it had finished its job and the water was ready. She grabbed a potholder and retrieved the kettle, expertly pouring scalding water over their bags. Jan went to the baking station she'd set up in the large kitchen to make searching for ingredients easier, and began to pull down the dry ingredients she needed for her new recipe—flour, baking soda and powder, ground cloves, salt, and sugar. Next, she would need to chop up pieces of pecan—she was eager to find out if the little brown flecks would look as wonderful against the pale-yellow backdrop of the muffin batter as she thought they would—and then she could get started on mixing the wet and dry ingredients together. Trying out a new recipe always made Jan feel like an artist—she could never tell if the outcome of her experiments would be a wonderful surprise, or a disaster. Part of the fun was the possibility that her next creation could be her very best.

A few minutes later, Elaine brought over her cup of tea as Jan poured the last of the remaining batter into an empty muffin cup. She popped the muffin tin into the oven and set a timer, then grabbed her tea, added a little sugar, and went over to join Elaine at the table so she could better see the television.

"Catch me up," Jan said as Rose sat down too.

"Well, this episode is about a forty-something guy whose father left him hundreds of old baseball cards. The brothers are consulting with an expert to see if any of them are worth anything, and then he'll have to decide by the end of the show whether he wants to sell the whole lot, some of them, or keep them," Elaine said.

"I always get a little teary when they decide to sell," Jan added. "I can understand wanting to let go of the clutter, especially if it's not something the person is interested in, and I can also understand the financial gain, but it always breaks my heart a little to see someone's prized possessions sifted through and sold off."

"I guess it does make you think how short life is. And anyway, we don't get to take any of our material things to heaven with us when our time comes, do we?" Elaine asked softly. Her cousin had a faraway look and seemed to be thinking of something else, and Jan wondered if it was the missing Camden statue.

"I know you have a lot of experience with letting go of things, what with Ben's career."

"Oh yes," Elaine said. "I learned quickly not to get too attached to anything." She grinned over the top of her tea-cup, then took a sip. "We never knew where Ben would get stationed the next time or whether or not something was too big or too-something to make the next trip. It was difficult sometimes, but it did teach me not to put too much value into stuff."

"I think that's a great lesson," Jan replied. "And one I could have used on an occasion or two. When you live in the same house for thirty years, it's amazing what can accumulate if you're not careful to clear things out regularly. And don't get me started on the kids' toys."

"Oh yeah," Elaine said. "I was forever having to get the kids to give up their old toys when they got new ones at Christmas or their birthdays, but that's not unique to military families. Anyone with more than one kid can sympathize with the toy home invasion." She winked at Jan.

"You had two to worry about, and the excuse of moving to get them to give stuff away," Jan said, chuckling. "Try three in a home they never had to move from."

Jan thought of her own children, Brian, Amy, and Tara, and then her grandchildren, thankful again that they lived fairly close by and she could see them regularly. It always bothered her that Elaine's kids weren't as near. She knew Elaine wished they were closer, but Elaine never complained about it. Jan had taken joy in the fact that her granddaughter Avery and Elaine were developing a friendship. Avery had struggled with some difficult girls in her school and Elaine had helped Avery build her confidence and stand up to them and they'd all been pleased when things had turned out okay, and the girls and Avery now got along.

Playing the cello had given Avery a unique skill she could be proud of. This along with her twice weekly gymnastics classes had shaped her into a lovely preteen on the verge of becoming a bright, hardworking young woman. Jan wondered what Kelly, Max, and Riley were up to, and made a mental note to give Brian and Amy each a call later.

"How is Avery, by the way?" Elaine asked.

"She's doing great. I think Paula said she's got a concert coming up that she's nervous about. I'll have to let her know she can come by here and play for the tearoom crowd."

"That's a great idea," Elaine said. "It will give her a chance to practice in front of a very forgiving audience."

"I'll do that," Jan said. "Avery would probably like that very much. Especially if I promise to reward her with cookies."

"*I* would play the cello for you if I knew I would get some of Jan's cookies out of it," Rose said, sending them all into a fit of giggles.

Though not a cello player, Rose was a talent in the kitchen, and she'd been doing very well in culinary school and had even begun dating a nice software engineer named Brent, whose wife had died of cancer several years before, leaving a young daughter to raise. It was wonderful to see Rose so happy and successful, but one of these days, Jan and Elaine both knew, the sweet young woman would finish her training, and she'd be on to bigger and better things.

"Speaking of cookies," Rose said, grinning, "my dad's been raving about your baking lately. What did you give him?"

Jan felt her cheeks warm and chastised herself for being so silly. Even after chatting with Elaine about Clifton, she still hadn't completely sorted out how she felt about the idea of him asking her out. Luckily, that hadn't happened yet, so she had some time still.

Elaine glanced over at Jan to see her reaction to Rose's innocent question.

"He must just really like the new recipes I've been trying lately," she said vaguely. "He seemed to especially enjoy those plum tarts I made the day he stopped by."

"He must," Rose said casually. "It's all he can talk about these days." She took a sip of her tea and focused her eyes back on the TV.

Jan was glad Rose didn't seem to think much about it— maybe she'd imagined the whole thing with Clifton after all. That would be something of a relief, she had to admit, because she definitely didn't need any drama in her life on top of Bob's leaving and the mixed emotions she'd been working to sort out since. Leave the drama to the television shows, she thought, turning back to the set as a commercial ended and the Henderson brothers appeared on-screen again.

The three women watched the rest of the half-hour program while enjoying their tea, adding in commentary here and there as the guy finally decided to sell some of his baseball cards and keep others—those he knew his father had loved the most—for sentimental value. When the segment concluded, only Gary and Stuart were left, but when Jan glanced at the clock to make sure they all got ready in time to open the tearoom, there were still a few minutes left until the closing credits. Jan decided to check on the muffins, whose excellent spice-and-citrus aroma had begun to infuse the kitchen, when Rose gave a sudden cry of excitement.

"What is it?" Jan asked. She'd bent over to pull the baked goods from the oven and could no longer see the television.

"You'll have to come over and see for yourself!" Elaine called. "Need any help with those muffins?"

Jan smiled to herself. "No, I'm fine here. I'll be over in a second."

Rose came to check on Jan, grasping her arm gently to lead her back to the table. "Watch this," Rose said.

"What is it? What's going on?" Jan sat as instructed, an oven mitt still on each hand, but she couldn't imagine what could possibly be so enthralling on a little semilocal antique show. But when she looked over to see if Elaine was as enamored as Rose, she saw her cousin's eyes glued to the screen, and if she wasn't mistaken, some of the color had drained from Elaine's face.

As she turned to watch, she heard the words that must have caused Elaine's sudden upset.

"Up until recently, the only plausible theory about its disappearance among experts was that the bronze likeness of the late Phillip Camden—seen only briefly since its commission—had somehow been destroyed. In the last few months, however, the rumor began that the statue had surfaced upon the death of the eccentric private collector, Jonathan Frost."

Jan couldn't believe her ears, and she looked over just in time to see Elaine's hand fly to her forehead.

"That's when things start to get mysterious," Stuart's voice blared from the TV, "because it remains unknown what happened to the statue following Mr. Frost's death. Things have been hush-hush surrounding the statue's whereabouts, but word is that it's in the care of the town of Lancaster. The problem is, no one has actually laid eyes on it yet, so whether or not it actually exists and where it's being kept remain a mystery."

"Though, as always, there are theories," Gary Henderson continued. "And that leads us to the topic of our next week's program. One of those theories, as Stuart mentioned, is that the statue may have ended up in Lancaster, Maine, the setting of much of Camden's most famous work."

The two brothers shared a furtive glance before Stuart spoke again. "So, next week, we'll be visiting none other than Lancaster to find out for ourselves what happened to the missing statue."

The three women looked at each other in astonishment. From her expression, Jan knew Rose was just excited to see a fairly famous television show paying notice to her little town. Elaine's features, however, showed a much different reaction.

"And of course we'll have special guests join us on our journey," Gary Henderson said from the screen. "The first will be Dr. Adam Watkins—a professor of literature at the University of Maine Augusta. Professor Watkins is one of the most esteemed academics studying Camden today."

The camera panned over to the back of a book cover with a photograph of a man on it, but it was too difficult to see from where Jan sat. Rose raised a hand to her face and put a finger to her lips as she moved nearer to the screen, her eyes narrowed as though she recognized something. Jan was just about to ask her when Stuart Henderson continued, "And our other guest will be none other than Jonathan Frost's only child, Miss Serina Frost."

The camera switched focus to a less-than-thrilled-looking woman with wavy dark hair and thick glasses with red, cat's-eye frames that took up the majority of her face. She seemed as nervous as Jan would feel if she had to appear on a television show, and the few seconds before the camera shifted away felt awkward as Serina Frost twitched nervously in her seat. Finally, the closing credits began to roll and the Henderson brothers signed off until next time.

Elaine was still speechless when the show ended, but Rose seemed to have figured out what she'd recognized before.

"I've seen that man," she said suddenly and loudly.

"Who?" Jan asked. "One of the Hendersons?"

Rose shook her head. "No, no, the other one—the professor. The one whose book they were showing."

"You've seen him where?" Elaine asked, obviously intrigued enough to pull out of her understandable stupor.

"At the library, I think," Rose answered, nodding. "Yes, that's it. When I went in the other day to check out a new recipe book I had put on hold."

Elaine's full attention was on their assistant now, and Jan was certain she was working to put a lead together.

"He was there, working at one of the computer tables, with a huge pile of books around him," Rose said. "I remember because I accidentally bumped into his chair and, when I apologized, he sort of waved me away without saying anything. I just thought it was a little odd and unfriendly at the time. Though it makes more sense now—maybe he's one of those super-focused academic types and just barely noticed what happened."

Elaine's eyes went wide, and she turned abruptly toward Jan. "You know what this means, don't you? It means that, in television time, since this was filmed last week, the crew should be here soon, if they aren't already."

"Probably keeping a low profile to avoid looky-loos," Rose said. "I know lots of people around here who'd be thrilled to get a close-up of a TV show set." She tossed back her ponytail and picked up her mug. With a quick gesture, she asked if Jan was finished with her tea as well.

"And that means," Elaine said, her mug of tea nearly untouched in front of her on the table, "we've just got wind of a possible motive."

"And," Jan chimed in, "a few more suspects too."

CHAPTER SEVEN

The morning became very busy very fast, as expected with all the buzz of a TV show coming to town, so Elaine and Jan didn't have much time to talk over the new information they'd discovered that morning. Elaine would make sure they sat down and rehashed what they knew this evening, after she gave Nathan a call to see how he was holding up. He'd been answering her texts with only short responses and seemed to have no time to talk.

She loved her job, but co-owning what was a popular tea-drinking, pastry-eating gathering place meant she wasn't always able to run off if the place was slammed, and she'd have to wait until the end of the working day to settle down and make some notes. That didn't mean, though, that she couldn't think about it here and there while she served customers.

As she bustled back and forth, bringing tea and pastries to visitors, and paced in and out of the kitchen door to reload on goodies, she made a mental list of what they knew so far. First, they were certain that the statue had been stolen, and hadn't simply disappeared. It seemed obvious, but sometimes it was best to start with the basics. If it had been a smaller, more portable object, the possibility of it being misplaced couldn't be ruled out. However, for obvious reasons, that wasn't the situation here. Second, Elaine knew that the statue was valuable—Nathan had spoken about it and Harrison had confirmed it when she and Jan had visited his shop. Third, she knew that only a handful of people were aware that it had been in Nathan's possession, including herself and Jan, whom she'd taken the liberty of ruling out on principle.

And now, she had this new material to sort through—the fact that Jonathan Frost had a daughter, who might not be too keen on her father bequeathing such a valuable possession to a town rather than his only living family member. Also, Professor Adam Watkins, whom Rose had seen at the library and who had been mentioned on that antiques-hunting TV show—a man who, presumably, somehow knew not only of the statue's existence, but also that it had been in Lancaster. Plus, the news that *Treasure Travels* was coming to her own little town to investigate the statue's whereabouts, which could not be a coincidence.

Some key questions rattled around in Elaine's mind. Did the hosts of *Treasure Travels*, and the guests of their next episode, know that the statue had been stolen? Or did they think they might find it when they came to town to do the show? And who were these guests, really? She needed to get her hands on a copy of Watkins's book, to find out what he'd discovered and written about the Camden statue, and she needed to ask Nathan if he'd read it—she assumed he probably had—and if he knew the professor personally. Then again, a historian like Watkins might have only intellectual and professional reasons to be interested in such a piece, so at the moment, Serina Frost's attention was much more suspicious. Her possible motive could be money related, and if Elaine had learned anything about crime, it was that money, or lack thereof, could be a powerful reason to do things a person shouldn't.

She felt a little better at the thought of looking further into the *Treasure Travels* cast and guests—but she knew it would do her good to sit down with Jan as soon as possible and rehash everything. Jan was just so good with the details, and she never missed a thing. Elaine was certain that if she told her cousin everything she'd just gone over, Jan would inevitably notice something she'd missed.

On that thought, she closed out the tabs of the afternoon's last remaining customers before heading back to the kitchen.

She passed Rose on her way in and smiled as the young woman carried an empty tray out into the hallway on her way to clear the last tables.

"Any stragglers?" Jan asked from near the dishwasher. Elaine shook her head as she set the tray full of dirty dishes on the counter. Jan eyed the tray. "I can fit the silverware in this load, but the plates and cups will have to wait till the next."

"That sounds good to me," Elaine said as she retrieved the dishwasher detergent from under the cabinet.

"Oh, thanks," Jan said. She put the soap into its little tray and shut the door before punching a few buttons to set the cycle.

Jan usually preferred to stay busy baking pastries, but the busy afternoon had required that she do other chores as well. Now, they were both pleasantly tired.

"Don't you love a good day's work?" Jan asked, grinning.

"Sure do," Elaine agreed, just as Rose pushed back through the door.

"Oh, I was going to get those," Rose said, unloading the dishes she'd brought back onto Elaine's tray, then setting her tray underneath.

"No, no," Jan argued. "You've got to get going before you miss your date with Brent."

Rose looked at her wristwatch. "That's right! I got so busy I almost forgot."

"Are you two doing anything special?" Elaine asked as she dug out all-purpose cleaner and began wiping down the counters where Jan had baked the day's pastries, as a quiet way to thank her cousin for handling the dishes. She liked the way they looked out for each other, rarely saying a word about it but pitching in when one part of the business got busier than others. Sometimes, Jan was overwhelmed with keeping enough pastries on hand, and Elaine would help by watching the timer and pulling things out of the oven, and it went back and forth. By now, they ran the tearoom like a well-oiled machine, and everyone seemed happy.

"Emma did very well on her most recent report card, so we're letting her choose what she wants for dinner, and then we're all going to make it together."

Elaine clasped her hands together. "That is perfect," she said as Jan made an *Aww* sound. "You guys are just the sweetest." She stopped herself from adding "little family" to the end of her statement, but it didn't keep her from thinking it. Rose had met her boyfriend at culinary school where he had enrolled to take a cooking class on how to make healthy food for his young daughter, Emma. Brent seemed to be doing everything he could to be a great single dad since his wife's death. When Rose had come along, Emma had really taken to her, and the three were fast becoming a family, if not officially just yet— though Elaine had high hopes that would change soon—then definitely in practice. Emma seemed to love having a woman around, and Rose and Brent got along wonderfully.

Rose beamed at her comment. "They really are a lot of fun," she said. "I'm starting to wonder what I'd do without them."

"Well, I know you'll be late if you don't get on out of here," Jan added, chuckling.

"All right, yes, I'll see you two in the morning," Rose called behind her as she headed for the hallway to grab her coat on the way out to her car.

Elaine and Jan heard a new voice just before the door closed behind Rose and, sharing a glance with her cousin, Elaine decided to go find out who it was. A quick look at the clock told her the tearoom was a half hour past closed, so she didn't think it would be new customers. A tired ache near her shoulders made her hope it wasn't, but she wouldn't turn away one last person.

"Hello there," she called into the hallway as she headed through the kitchen door. As she got closer to the front door, she caught the silhouette of a woman standing there, still wearing her coat, scarf, and gloves as if uncertain what to do next. "Can I help you with something?"

"Oh, hi," the woman said softly. When she turned around, Elaine was hit with a sense of recognition, but she couldn't quite identify it.

"My name is Geraldine and, well, I've been playing phone tag with Jan Blake," she said, the statement lifting up at the end in question.

The woman was some years older than Elaine and Jan, with neatly styled soft gray hair and lovely hazel eyes. She carried herself with an air of quiet confidence, though Elaine saw hints of uncertainty in her eyes, and there was a familiarity in her features that Elaine was not able to place.

"Of course," Elaine said, reaching out to take Geraldine's offered hand, from which she had removed a glove. "I remember. You were interested in coming by again, to see about a painting."

Geraldine nodded. "Yes, that's right."

"Here, let me take your coat," Elaine offered, hanging it carefully on the rack when the woman obliged. "Would you like to come in and have a cup of tea?"

Geraldine looked around at the empty parlors. "I would love to, but it seems I've come after business hours once again and I don't want to put you out."

Elaine shook her head. "Nonsense. It's no bother at all."

Geraldine's eyes warmed. "Well, in that case, if you're certain."

"I am," Elaine said, taking her elbow to lead her into the kitchen. "Though I hope you don't mind a little less formality than we usually show our customers."

"Not at all," Geraldine said. As they walked, she asked, "In one of her phone message responses to me, Ms. Blake mentioned a man named Archie Bentham, who has a connection to the painting. Does he happen to be here today?"

"He's not at the moment, but let me give him a call to see if he could come by. He lives not far from here."

"Oh no, I couldn't ask you to do that," Geraldine objected, stopping in the hallway outside the kitchen door just as Jan peeked out to see what was going on.

"Jan, you remember Geraldine?" Elaine asked.

"Oh yes, hello again." Jan said, holding the door open as the two women passed through, then letting it swing shut behind the three of them. "I'm so sorry that we've been playing phone tag since then and haven't been able to catch each other."

"Oh, that's just how it goes sometimes," Geraldine said. Elaine led her to the table and pulled out a chair. "I really do not want to impose," she added, slightly nervously. "I should have called, but I was in the area and thought I'd stop by."

"It's really okay," Elaine said. "Let me just step out to call Archie. I'm sure he would like to speak with you about the painting. Please, just wait here while I call him."

Geraldine nodded and Elaine excused herself, hearing Jan offering tea as she stepped into the hallway and pulled her cell phone out of her pocket. As the phone rang, she recalled Geraldine's previous visit, which had come about because of a painting they'd discovered.

Archie had recognized his father's unique monogram on the painting from his letters and notes. Until that time, Archie hadn't any clue that his father had been a painter because he'd always gone off to an office each day to work as a government clerk. When they took the piece to Heather Wells for repair, she'd informed them it wasn't the original frame, which was much newer than the painting itself. Heather had also suspected that the signature was that of a famous painter, Harley Archibald Benningham, but she did not feel qualified to say for certain. Following up on Heather's recommendation, Nathan had suggested Elaine send the painting to be authenticated by an art historian in New York, who currently still had the painting.

The whole situation had been startling to poor Archie, who'd never seen any of his father's paintings.

Elaine heard a click and the phone ceased its ringing. "Hello?" Archie said on the other end.

"Hi, Archie, it's Elaine. Do you remember some time back when you saw a woman who looked like your father leaving the tearoom?"

"Yes," he said, sounding flustered. "I do remember."

"Well, that very woman is here at the tearoom again," Elaine continued. "I've persuaded her to stay until you can get here. I hate to bother you on your day off, but would you be able to stop by to see her? She seemed awfully disappointed when she learned that you weren't here and I'd be hard pressed to send her away."

"Of course," Archie said. Elaine could hear noises in the background that made it sound like he was getting ready. "Just give me a moment and I'll be right there."

She breathed a sigh of relief. "Thank you."

They hung up and Elaine tucked the phone back into her pocket before returning to the kitchen. Jan had already provided Geraldine with a cup of tea and one of the orange clove muffins that had been a hit that morning with the customers, and Elaine sat down at the table to join in their chatter.

It wasn't much later when they heard Archie's pickup pull in and he appeared through the kitchen door.

"I'm so sorry to keep you waiting," he said by way of greeting when Geraldine stood up. "Do we know each other from somewhere?"

"I'm not certain, but I don't think so."

The two shook hands and Geraldine introduced herself before Elaine led them back to the kitchen table. "Jan and I should probably head upstairs," she offered, but Geraldine shook her head.

"There's no need to do that. I'd love for the two of you to stay and chat. Ms. Blake, you were so kind before when I came here to track down the painting and I'd hate for you to feel you have to leave."

Elaine and Jan shared a glance before sitting back down.

"It's lovely to meet you, Geraldine," Archie said.

"You too." Her brow knit as she looked around at all of them in turn, holding tightly to her cup of English breakfast tea. "I have to tell you...I feel drawn here, somehow, as if I've got some kind of connection to this place." Geraldine seemed to be struggling to explain herself. "I must sound silly," she added softly, looking down into her lap.

"No, not at all," Elaine said. "We just wish there was more we could do to help you."

"There is something that might help," Geraldine said.

Elaine nodded and Archie leaned in, curious.

"I know you mentioned that the painting was being authenticated," she said to Jan. "But would you happen to have a picture of the painting? Just so I could set my mind at rest as to whether it's the one my son accidentally gave away?"

"Sure," Jan said, smiling. "I've got a copy on hand. I know it's not the same as seeing the real thing, but you're welcome to have a look. I'm so glad we were able to make a copy so that at least you can see what it looks like."

Geraldine's face lit up at the news. Elaine could only imagine the woman's delight at finally having a chance to look at it—even if it wasn't the painting itself.

They all rose from the table, Geraldine leaving her tea, and headed to the west parlor where it hung in place of the real thing.

"Here it is," Elaine said.

Geraldine gave a little gasp and leaned in to study the domestic scene trapped between her hands, and Elaine, Jan, and Archie did the same from over her shoulders, careful not to crowd her.

The painting portrayed a woman seated at a table inside the sunny room of an apartment. On the table's surface rested a bouquet of flowers in varying shades of soft pinks and purples, alongside a steaming cup of tea. That very cup of tea had been what initially drew Elaine to the painting, and she and Jan both felt it would be a wonderful addition to their growing collection of parlor decorations. The woman in the painting had brown hair that was styled into a knot on the base of her neck, and she faced away from the viewer as if gazing out of the window. One didn't need a full view of the woman's face to get the sense that she was very pretty, and Elaine wondered again who she might be.

Geraldine stood very still, transfixed by the scene. Elaine and Jan had spoken at length of how it was one of those paintings that a person simply couldn't look away from—its beauty just drew you in and made you want to be a part of the scene, enjoying the view outside the window of the cozy room.

"It's just as I remember," Geraldine said, echoing Elaine's thoughts as the woman held it up to her face and peered at it even more closely. Elaine thought she might have seen a glisten in Geraldine's eyes.

Geraldine stared in wonder, then looked up, confusion and other not-so-clear emotions warring in her features.

"Is something wrong?" Archie asked. He looked like he wished to comfort her but wasn't sure how to do so.

Geraldine scrunched up her nose. "It's as I said when I came before—I distinctly recall it hanging above my bed as a girl, and I've had it with me, but stored away, for many years. When I moved to the retirement community, my son was helping me, and—well, he cleared out what he thought was old rubbish. It wasn't really his fault that he gave it away. But I'm positive this is the very same painting."

Archie studied her closely. "Where did you grow up?" he asked.

Geraldine tilted her head a little to one side. "Now, that is a complicated story if ever there was one."

Elaine was intrigued, and, if she knew her cousin, Jan's expression indicated she was too.

"Shall we return to the table and sit down?" Jan asked.

Geraldine had a faraway look in her eye but gave a little nod. "Yes, that sounds good," she said.

Once they were back at the table, Elaine offered to refresh Geraldine's cup of tea and get the others one as well. She listened to their soft chatter as she boiled water and got out the bags, thinking how large a role tea had in all their lives. She had long since come to appreciate the tradition of a nice warm cup, and it seemed to make any situation more tolerable, even the most difficult. Not only that, but it brought people together, which was, she felt, its most important quality. Finally, the kettle was ready, and she brought over a tray with fresh cups, bags, sugar, and milk, along with some pecan sandies.

As Elaine served the other three, she heard Geraldine answer Archie's earlier question.

"I was adopted and raised by a Yorkshire family. They were wonderful to me," she said, but then her voice grew quieter. "I tried later to learn more about my adoption, but not until I was well into adulthood. I felt guilty. My adoptive parents were the best a girl could have asked for—I didn't want them to think I wished for…something else."

Elaine, Archie, and Jan all nodded as Geraldine's words touched their hearts.

"But eventually, curiosity got the better of me and I started to look into it. Sadly, and, most frustratingly, I didn't get very far."

They looked at her in question, hanging on to her every word. "There seems to be no record of my adoption at all. It's almost as if I didn't exist until my parents decided to take me in."

The three of them listened as Geraldine told what little else she could of her story, and a long silence followed.

"No one has mentioned this to you before today, but—" Archie paused and swallowed, glancing at Jan and Elaine, who nodded encouragingly to him. "We—and more than one art expert—think that the painting was likely done by my father."

Geraldine blinked. "Your father? He was an artist?"

Archie nodded. "We think he painted under the name Harley Archibald Benningham, although his real name was Henry Arthur Bentham. I did not know he had been an artist until Elaine here stumbled across the painting. But I recognized his mark, here." Archie indicated the interlocked initials on the print before them on the table.

"Do you think my birth parents might have purchased the painting from him?" Geraldine asked, looking bewildered.

Archie cleared his throat. Elaine sent up a silent prayer that what she suspected he was about to say would not be taken the wrong way. "When you were here before, I mentioned to Jan that you closely resemble someone I knew. My father." Archie paused, seemingly to select his words with extra attentiveness. "Do you think," he asked carefully, "that my father could have been...I mean, is it possible that your birth father may have been...my father?"

Geraldine swallowed heavily. Her eyes widened as she worked over the new idea. "I suppose it's possible."

After a few seconds in which the air in the kitchen became thick with palpable intensity as everyone pondered Archie's suggestion, Elaine asked if anyone would like some cookies with their tea.

"Oh," Geraldine said quickly, glancing at the cookies, "I'm so sorry to tell you this because those pecan sandies look absolutely wonderful, but I'm allergic."

"I'm so sorry," Elaine said, moving to switch out the cookies for a different dessert, but Geraldine held up a palm to stop her.

"Please don't trouble yourself," Geraldine added. "The tea alone will be perfect."

Something flashed in Archie's hazel eyes—eyes, Elaine noticed suddenly, that looked strikingly similar to Geraldine's.

"I think I may be allergic to pecans too," he said. "Pecan pie has always bothered me something awful the few times I've had it at Christmas. I've learned to avoid it, and they're not in season too often, so when Jan bakes anything with those particular nuts, I just steer clear, but I've never gotten any official testing done to confirm a diagnosis."

It was then that all motion in the room ceased as the four adults simultaneously reached the same conclusion.

CHAPTER EIGHT

"That was something else, wasn't it?" Jan asked Elaine after Geraldine and Archie left. The two had decided to continue their conversation over dinner at a restaurant, and Jan and Elaine had declined the offer to join them, both hoping that Archie and Geraldine would get a chance to know one another better.

"It was almost as if you could feel their connection," Elaine said.

It was just after six and Jan and her cousin were out on the screened porch. Jan was sweeping up the last bit of the morning's mild snowfall while Elaine cleaned Earl Grey's litter box.

"Do you really think it's possible that they are siblings?" Jan asked, pausing the broom midair as she thought of what that would mean to Archie.

"Well, God works in mysterious ways," Elaine quoted. "I would say just about anything is possible."

"Wouldn't it be strange to find out that you had a brother or a sister so late in life?"

Elaine looked up from where she'd crouched in Earl Grey's corner restroom area. "Strange, yes, but it could also be wonderful."

"I just can't imagine. If it's true, that means Archie's father led a whole different life before Archie ever came into the picture."

Elaine nodded. "That wasn't so unusual during the war. A lot of families got separated when soldiers went off to fight. Sometimes when they came back, there wasn't anyone left."

"It's so sad to think about," Jan said. "You must have been so thankful every time Ben survived an assignment and came home to you."

"Yes, I was." Elaine smiled wistfully. "I prayed for him every day each time he was gone—even if it was just for a day's mission—and I prayed for him every day I had him at home with me."

If Archie and Geraldine were related, it would be their decision whether or not to sort out the details. And if Jan knew anything, it was that God worked things out in His own time, whether His children found it challenging or not.

Elaine finished clearing out the litter box and took the garbage out. When she returned, she glanced at her watch. "I've got to meet Nathan over at Dan Benson's office in half an hour—we're going to go over our statements and sign them."

Jan nodded. "I don't have any plans. Is there anything I can do to help?"

"As a matter of fact, there is," Elaine said. She bit her bottom lip. "The library is open late tonight, right?"

"I think so," Jan said.

"If it's not too much trouble, do you think you could stop by there and speak to Priscilla for me?"

"Sure, I don't see why not," Jan said, brushing the last of the snow out through the porch door. "What is it you need to find out from her?"

Elaine held the door open for Jan and then followed her inside. The kitchen was warm and inviting, but Jan was too eager to help her cousin to want to sit down and soak it in. That would come later in the evening, and then she might want to visit her craft room to pick up where she'd left off her latest sewing project. It would be a nice quiet respite after what was turning out to be a long day full of surprises.

"I want to know if the police found anything on the security footage they picked up from the night of the theft."

Jan wrinkled her brow. "I don't at all mind helping, but won't you be at Dan's anyway, with Nathan? Can't you ask Dan then?"

Elaine looked the slightest bit guilty for a passing second. "I'm reluctant to because of my relationship with Nathan."

"Are the police still considering him a suspect?"

"Dan hasn't said if they've ruled him out yet, and I haven't been able to really talk to him."

"Does he have an alibi?" Jan felt the question was put casually, but she was surprised when Elaine flushed a warm shade of pink.

"He told Dan he was at the library the afternoon the statue was stolen, then went straight home," Elaine said, sounding like she was embarrassed but didn't think she should be.

Jan stopped and turned to face her cousin. They shared a look, but Jan didn't say anything.

"I know what it looks like," Elaine said quietly. "It's pretty hard to prove that you were home if you were the only one there. Add to that the fact that I couldn't reach him that night."

"It's not that," Jan reassured her cousin. "I'm worried about you, and that he hasn't told you why he wouldn't answer your texts or phone calls that night. It seems like he might be hiding something and I just don't want you to be hurt."

Elaine's expression was hard to read. "I trust him, Jan," she said emphatically. "I know he didn't steal the statue. It wouldn't make sense for him to do so, at any rate, but the most important thing is, I know he loves me."

Jan put a hand on her cousin's shoulder. "I'm sure everything will work out."

After a few moments, Elaine's color returned to normal and she looked a little less worried.

"So, tell me," Jan said, changing the subject. "What else do you want me to talk to Priscilla about?"

"I want you to ask Priscilla if you can look at the mannequin that was left in place of the statue. If she allows you to, try to take a photo of it. I meant to when we discovered the theft, but Dan Benson was there and I didn't want to seem too nosy."

Jan nodded. "I also need to know if she has any copies of that book," Elaine added.

"What book?"

When Elaine answered, Jan thought she looked like herself again—resolved to see this through and ready to get to work. "The one that professor wrote. What was his name?"

"Oh yes," Jan said, snapping her fingers as she recalled the episode of *Treasure Travels*. "Watkins!"

"That's it," Elaine confirmed. "Adam Watkins. If she has a copy of that book, please check it out. We want to see if there's anything in there that might have led someone to believe they could find and take that statue."

"HEY THERE, PRISCILLA," Jan called as she entered Lancaster Public Library.

Priscilla Gates looked up from the front desk, on top of which was scattered a pile of intimidating-looking papers. "Oh, hi, Jan," the librarian said, grinning. "How are you these days? I haven't seen you in here in a while." She took her reading glasses off and set them on top of the stack, which appeared dangerously close to toppling over.

"I'm fine, but you're right, I haven't been by in a long time." Jan glanced around. "But I couldn't stay away from the smell of books for too long."

"I'd be lying if I said that smell wasn't one of the best parts of the job."

Jan giggled. She and shy Priscilla had become friends, and Jan always enjoyed the librarian's gentle company.

"Though the smells that come with your job are a close second, I'm sure," Priscilla added.

"It'd be false modesty for me to disagree with you," Jan said, thinking of the pleasure she took in baking.

"So tell me, how can I help you?" Priscilla asked, folding her hands.

"First, I want to say I'm sorry about what happened the other day, and to let you know that Elaine and I are doing our best to figure out what happened to that statue."

Priscilla's mouth formed a thin line. "Yes, it's awful," she said. "I keep hoping it will just turn up, but we're all still waiting to see what happens. And, of course, everyone keeps asking me if we're still going to have the fund-raiser."

"Are you?" Jan asked.

Priscilla shook her head. "It's tempting to cancel after what happened."

"But do you have other plans for it? As a backup, I mean?"

The librarian briefly rolled her eyes toward the ceiling. "I wish, and normally, we absolutely would. But we only have a short time before the fund-raiser. And once Nathan told me he had something special to present that would mean so much to the library and to this community, I decided not to plan anything else. He made it sound as if this surprise presentation would draw more attention than we've had in years, and"—she pointed down at the large mound of work beneath her elbows—"it's far too late now. I'm in the middle of annual inventory and I've got way too much to do to plan more attractions for the fund-raiser this late in the game."

Jan nodded, realizing how bad this looked for Nathan. Not only did the statue mean a great deal to him, but it seemed he'd also made a promise he ended up being unable to keep. Her heart sank at the thought of his predicament.

Priscilla let out a little sigh. "But who's to say if I'd planned out a whole bunch of entertainment that we wouldn't have had a blizzard or something anyway, right? That's life, I guess." She looked up at Jan. "But it might make me feel better if I can help a patron."

Jan returned Priscilla's friendly grin. "There are two things," she said.

"Even better." Priscilla winked. "Let's start with the first."

"Well, I'd like to see the mannequin, if that's all right with you." Jan fully expected Priscilla to ask her reason, but the librarian just nodded. She and her cousin were developing a not-bad reputation as local sleuths, and with their solve rate, Jan thought happily, it made sense that people wouldn't be too hesitant to accept their help. She wasn't one to look a gift horse—or mannequin—in the mouth.

"I don't see why not," Priscilla said, grabbing a key from a drawer under the counter and coming around through the little gate to join Jan. "Follow me."

She led Jan to the storage room and opened up the door. "There you go," she said, waving an arm at a figure that was laid out on a long table, looking unpleasantly like a dead body, albeit one dressed in outdoor work clothes.

Jan had a sudden thought and frowned. "Shouldn't the police have taken it in as evidence?"

Priscilla shook her head. "They said they didn't need to because they'd already dusted it for fingerprints and taken photographs. I promised I'd leave it here as is and, I should say as a friendly reminder, not allow anyone to touch it, so they decided to leave it here till Ellerby can retrieve it."

"I guess that makes sense," Jan said. "And I promise I won't touch it. I would, though," she added tentatively, "like to take a photo for Elaine if you don't mind."

"Sure, that seems okay with me. The police didn't say anything against it."

"Okay, thanks," Jan said, pulling her cell out of her pocket. She adjusted the flash settings to accommodate the dimly lit room and took a series of snapshots from different sides and angles. "That should do," she said when she'd finished. "Thanks again, Priscilla."

"Don't thank me," the librarian said as they returned to the checkout desk. "Just let me know if you and Elaine come up with anything. I'd love to stay in the loop so I can let the board members know whether we can keep the fund-raiser scheduled."

"Will do," Jan agreed. She adjusted her purse on her shoulder. "There's something else..."

"*Mmm-hmm?*" Priscilla mumbled absentmindedly, seeming to be overwhelmed again at the sight of her stacks of papers.

"Do you by any chance happen to have any copies of a book by a Dr. Adam Watkins?"

Priscilla looked up at the ceiling, thinking. Jan knew the librarian had her very own card catalog inside her bright mind and could probably list on request almost any book from the library's inventory.

Priscilla held up a finger. "As a matter of fact, I do," she concluded. "It's fairly new. In fact, I think it's only been published for about a month, give or take a week."

"Great," Jan said. "I'd love to check it out if it's not on hold."

Priscilla pulled up the computer database while Jan pulled out her wallet and found her library card.

"Nope, you're in luck; it's not on hold," she said, sounding pleased. "Though I can't say I'm not surprised. I would have thought more local amateur historians would be interested in reading Watkins's thoughts on the mysterious past of the Camden statue."

"I read a little online about Watkins," Jan said, "and from what I saw, it seemed he might be something of an eccentric. I got the sense he's not taken too seriously among other Camden scholars."

"Ah, I see," Priscilla said. "Let me just go grab that and I'll be right back."

Jan browsed a shelf of new releases near the front desk, and thought about grabbing one whose cover caught her eye, before she remembered all the sewing projects she'd started and not yet had a chance to finish. Another time, she promised herself, she would come back and get something fat and escapist to read. But for now, she and Elaine had bigger fish to fry.

Priscilla returned with the book and scanned its barcode before placing a little slip behind the front cover. "Here you are," she said. "I hope you enjoy it, even if it does turn out to be controversial."

The librarian passed the thick hardback volume over the counter and Jan accepted it. Elaine would have to skim the heavy thing, otherwise she'd be in for a long night.

"I'll be sure to let you know," Jan said. "And don't worry, Elaine and I will keep you in the loop."

"That would be most helpful," Priscilla said, giving Jan a thankful smile.

She happened to glance up at a little black lens near the front door and had a thought. "Oh, Priscilla. One more thing."

"What is it?"

"Do you know if the police found anything on the security camera recordings from the night the statue was taken?"

Priscilla's eyes widened and she shook her head. "It's the most irritating thing," she said. "They said the camera wasn't on that night—someone must have tampered with it and turned it off. I can't imagine who would be able to do that, though."

Jan thanked the librarian once more before heading out the front door, her head spinning with new evidence, none of which, unfortunately, seemed to fit together.

ELAINE MET NATHAN at Dan Benson's home so they could sign their statements. Dan greeted them at the front door, then walked them to his family's dining room, where they each sat while the other went into Dan's office to go over the documents he had typed up after interviewing them at the library. Elaine read through and signed hers in just a few moments since Dan's notes were thorough and accurate. When it was Nathan's turn, she couldn't help but notice, glancing nervously at the clock every few moments, that Dan spent a greater amount of time with Nathan than he had with her, and she tried not to read too much into that realization.

When the two men emerged from the office a half hour later, she practically jumped out of her seat. Nathan seemed eager to leave, so they said a quick goodbye to Dan and walked out into the chilly evening air.

"Would you like to grab a bite to eat before you head home?" Elaine asked, pausing as they reached their cars parked along the curb. Instead of picking her up from the tearoom as he usually did, Nathan had suggested they take separate cars to Dan's, mumbling something about having an errand afterward. But now she tried again, hoping he might relax a little if they had a nice meal and some time together.

Nathan looked down at his feet, seeming to avoid her eyes. "I'd love to, but I've got to get going," he said, his tone difficult to read. "How about another time?"

Elaine nodded and put on a little smile, but inside she was a tiny bit hurt that he didn't seem to want her company. She hesitated before deciding to just come out with her true feelings. "Nathan, I know you're not responsible for what happened, but I have to say—you're acting strange."

He looked up at her with uncharacteristic irritation. "You're right. I'm not responsible, and I resent being made to feel as though I did something wrong."

Elaine swallowed before speaking again, more gently than she felt. "If you'd only tell me why you didn't contact me right away the night the statue was taken, and why you've been so short and vague in your calls and texts lately, maybe everything would be clear and we could let this go and find out who really did it."

He looked at her then and sighed, his eyes filled with sadness and fatigue. If only he would open up to her, she knew she could help.

"I trust you, Nathan. I know you didn't do this," she said, reaching out to squeeze his hand as they both shivered, the late-evening air growing colder by the minute.

"Thank you," he responded, weariness clouding his voice. "I would never take that statue for myself. It's one of the neatest things I've ever had the privilege of handling, and I love this town. I wouldn't take away the pleasure of having that statue here, where it belongs, from the community I care about."

There was nothing but sincerity in his words, and Elaine believed him.

And yet a question still lingered at the back of her mind.

"So why didn't you text me back that night until almost an hour later?" she asked tentatively.

"I just didn't feel like answering my phone, okay?" he snapped, his breath clouding as the temperature continued to drop. Immediately, his features filled with remorse. "I'm sorry, Elaine," he said sadly. "I didn't mean to sound unkind."

At that she let the subject drop, not wanting to upset him further. She knew that something was wrong, but she hoped he would tell her when he felt the time was right.

CHAPTER NINE

The next morning was Sunday, so Elaine and Jan got to "sleep in," as they jokingly referred to waking a couple of hours later to go to church than they usually did to start a workday.

They shared a quick breakfast of pastries left over from Saturday's baking, then put on their warm gear and left the house, glad the overnight snow hadn't blocked the drive. The roads were reasonably clear as they traveled the short distance to Lancaster Community Church. Elaine enjoyed seeing its steeple rising above town, a beacon to guide believers and seekers alike to the traditional white clapboard building underneath. The sight of it comforted her in weary times, and reminded her that God was always there—if one simply remembered to look up.

As Jan drove, Elaine thought back to the tense evening she'd had with Nathan. It was by far the most difficult situation the two had undergone as a couple, and seeing Nathan in pain tore at her heart. But she tried to focus her eyes on God's promise that His plan was a good one, and that there was a reason for each trial they might face—and face this they would—together.

Her mind back in the present as Jan continued to drive, Elaine looked out the window, admiring the simple, rustic beauty of freshly fallen snow weighing down the trees and brush that grew alongside the road, and even the silvery, cloud-covered sky above that promised yet again more snow. Though it proved challenging even for the toughest northerners, there was something to be said about its consistency. No matter what happened, the snow would fall in the winter, and there was a season for everything. She said a silent prayer of thanks for that, and for the faces of the friends she saw as Jan pulled the car into the church parking lot.

The two women got out and greeted their community members and, on their way in, Pastor Mike. Finding her regular seat, Elaine sat down and put her purse under the pew. She leaned forward to tap Annie Richardson on the shoulder. The two women visited for a few minutes and Elaine asked after the dairy farm Annie and her husband, Gavin, owned and operated together. She and Jan often bought baking supplies— eggs, milk, and cream—from them, and they were never disappointed in the quality of the fresh goods. Annie's children joined their mother after talking with their friends and then the sanctuary quieted down as it was time for the service to begin.

Elaine glanced around quickly and spotted Avery; Jan's preteen granddaughter gave her a little wave. Brian and Paula had come by to spend time with Jan, and Elaine had arranged with Avery and her parents to take Avery out to lunch after church. Jan was going to drop them off at Kate's Diner after the service, and Elaine was looking forward to spending time with the girl. They spent a lot of time together and Elaine thoroughly enjoyed her company.

She often missed her own children and grandchildren, who all lived far away, and Avery's role in her life had helped a great deal to ease that loneliness for family.

Elaine turned toward the front as Jan sat next to her and the service began. Pastor Mike taught from Joshua 1:9, "Have not I commanded thee? Be strong and of a good courage; be not afraid, neither be thou dismayed: for the Lord thy God is with thee whithersoever thou goest." It was the perfect reminder that morning and Elaine wondered again at the greatness of the Lord, and at His ability to speak directly to her in her time of need. She made a mental note to share the passage with Nathan when she saw him again. She hoped it would bring him the same peace it had brought her.

After the last hymn and benediction, she and her cousin gathered their handbags and made their way to the door, a process which, not unpleasantly, took ages, since they had to visit with all of their friends. When at last they reached Avery's family's pew, Avery came up and hugged Elaine and Jan.

"Hi, dear, how are you today? Did you enjoy youth group?"

Avery nodded and gave a little summary of what they'd talked about in class. Then she said goodbye to her family and followed Jan and Elaine out to the car.

"How's school going?" Jan asked on the way.

"Oh, it's pretty good," Avery said.

"Are those girls still treating you well?" Jan asked, referring to a bullying situation from a while back that had thankfully been resolved.

"Yes, and we pretty much all get along fine now."

Jan smiled at Elaine.

"You've got a concert coming up with a solo, I hear," Elaine said. "Feeling good about it?"

Avery swallowed. "Um, I think it's going to be okay. Dad says I just have to keep practicing."

Elaine heard the concern creeping into the girl's voice and her heart went out to her. "I think you're so brave for having a solo. I know it's a lot of responsibility, but I can't think of a better person to handle it." She gave Avery's shoulder a gentle squeeze and opened the car door for the child.

"Oh, thank you," she said politely. "It's not so bad. I just get a little nervous in front of people, that's all."

"Well, I think I know how to work on that," Jan said. "Why don't you give us a little preview later, and we'll try our best to look like the harshest critics you can think of."

"That sounds like a pretty good idea, Grandma," Avery said through giggles, her blue eyes bright and her golden hair shining in the single ray of sun that had managed to find its way through the thick clouds. Sometimes when Avery laughed, it reminded Elaine that, while she was on the verge of becoming a teenager, she was still a little girl at heart. "But maybe not the harshest. Just a little harsh."

Elaine laughed. She loved that kid's spunk and the funny things she said when she forgot the angst of being her age and remembered to be herself.

"Deal," Jan said, starting up the car.

Avery caught them up on the gymnastics classes she took twice a week at the Boys and Girls Club and on what she was reading in English and studying in science class, making a show of fake gagging when she got to the part about possibly having to dissect a frog soon. Just the thought made Elaine queasy and she hoped something else would replace the idea in her mind before they sat down to lunch.

"I think I remember my friend Stephanie being absent from school the day we had to dissect frogs, with a 'flu' that cleared up suspiciously fast," Jan said, chuckling. "I went ahead and came to class, but I don't recall enjoying it."

"*Eww*, me neither," Elaine chimed in. "Your friend had a good plan. I wish I'd thought of that."

"But don't get any ideas," Jan said, feigning sternness as she glanced at Avery in the rearview mirror. Avery rolled her eyes as Elaine looked back, then she winked.

"I won't, Grandma," she said. "Besides, I think it'll be interesting to see what's going on in there."

Elaine shuddered, but she admired the girl's brave attitude and her curious mind. Avery had struggled with confidence in the recent past, but each day she grew more and more sure of herself, while staying sweet and humble. It was as much a joy to watch her grow as it was her own grandchildren. Ever since moving in with Jan and starting Tea for Two, it felt like she had gained closeness with Jan's side of the family, and she loved that. If only she could get her own kids to move closer.

But she reminded herself to be thankful for the gifts she'd been given.

Jan pulled into the parking lot at Kate's Diner. "All right, gals. I'll be back to pick you up in an hour." She winked at

Elaine over her shoulder, then caught Avery's eye. "Don't get into too much trouble, now."

Avery laughed. "We'll try to," she joked.

"See you later, Jan," Elaine said. "Thanks again for the ride."

Her cousin nodded and pulled back out onto the road.

"I hope you're hungry," Elaine said, taking Avery's shoulder. "I know I am."

"I love the food here, but I can never decide what I want. I still like some of the stuff on the kids' meal, but I'm getting into the regular menu too."

Elaine grinned. "Whereas I sometimes wish I could order off the kids' meal."

Avery laughed. "But you're too old!"

"Indeed," Elaine said. "But that doesn't stop me from wanting to."

"You should do it and see what they say," Avery prodded, making Elaine laugh.

"Maybe I'll try that sometime, but I'd better not do it today and risk us getting kicked out when I'm just about starving."

Avery giggled and held open the door for Elaine, a display of politeness that made Elaine proud. As soon as they entered, the smell of freshly grilled hamburgers hit Elaine's nose, and she forgot all about the kid's menu.

"Well, hello there, ladies," a woman's voice called from near the middle of the large room. "How's it going today?"

Kate Pierce, the owner, walked over to greet Elaine and Avery, then handed them each a menu and showed them to a table near the front window, where they had a view of the lake and, in the distance, Macy's Green Glade Cottages. Kate, a die-hard Pittsburgh Steelers fan, wore her customary scarf with the team's logo on it, and her dark eyes were lively as she asked them for their drink orders.

Elaine thought for sure Avery would go for a soda, but instead, she chose chocolate milk.

"Good choice," Kate said. "Keep those growing bones strong." She jotted down the order, then turned to Elaine. "And for you?"

"While chocolate milk sounds delightful, I think I'll just have a water for now," Elaine said.

Kate smiled and asked if they were ready to choose food. Avery nodded and requested a grilled cheese sandwich, and Elaine, vowing to have a more virtuous salad for dinner, picked a burger decked out with mushrooms, goat cheese, and pesto, her mouth watering even as she placed the order.

"Okay, girls," Kate said, pocketing her pad and pen. "I'll tell Patti and we'll get these right out to you."

Patti Garland and Lydia Pierce were Kate's two daughters, who helped her run the busy restaurant that stayed open year-round for breakfast and lunch. It was a mainstay for Lancaster residents, especially in the dead of winter, when practically everything else shut down. Folks who wanted to go out for a good meal they didn't have to cook themselves could do so, and with a hefty side helping of local gossip besides. Elaine and Jan loved Kate's generous portions and the simple but creative and, most importantly, delicious offerings.

Elaine and Avery admired the view and worked on the crossword puzzle that decorated the paper kids' menu Avery had asked for, just in case, and it wasn't long before Lydia brought over their beverages. Ten minutes later, their food arrived, and they tucked into it happily, eating in companionable silence.

Finally, Avery put down the last little piece of her sandwich and took a sip of her milk, then looked at Elaine earnestly. "So, I know we were joking about it earlier, but I'm really struggling with that cello solo. I just didn't want to worry Grandma about it because she'd tell my mom, and my mom already worries about me plenty as it is."

Elaine looked at Avery with a serious expression. "She worries about you because she loves you. You know that, don't you?"

Avery grabbed a french fry and swirled it around in the sauce she'd mixed of mayonnaise, mustard, and ketchup. "Yes," she said, then was quiet for a moment. "But I wish she wouldn't so much, you know?" She looked up at Elaine in question. "It's hard to try to be good at something when you know someone really wants you to be good at it, if that makes sense."

Elaine nodded. "It does."

Avery waved the fry in the air. "It's like, if no one expected me to be good at cello, then I'd have more room to *be* good at cello."

"I think you're saying you'd feel more comfortable if there wasn't any pressure."

"Exactly," Avery said, dunking the fry back into the sauce before eating it.

"I can understand that, but sometimes a little pressure pushes us to do our best."

Avery tilted her head and narrowed her eyes. "But if no one expected you to be good, it wouldn't matter if you weren't good."

Elaine grinned. "That's right. So, if it didn't matter, you probably wouldn't do it then, would you?"

The young girl thought about that idea for a moment. "I guess that does kind of make sense," she concluded. "It's challenging because it matters, and it matters because it's challenging."

"Something like that," Elaine said, nodding. She wiped her hands on her napkin and took a sip of her water. "The things that we find challenging are often the very things that give us confidence when we accomplish them. When we're able to succeed at something we initially thought we could never do very well, it feels good, and it makes us believe we can do other difficult things."

Avery bit her lower lip and began to nod. "Yeah, that's true. I never thought of it like that before."

Elaine smiled, glad she could help.

"I guess I just don't want to be embarrassed in front of everyone—or to embarrass my family—if I don't do a good job on the solo. Like, it's different if I'm part of the whole group and we don't do well. With the solo, it's all on me for a few minutes, so if I mess up, it's totally my fault."

"While that may be, your instructor would not have given the solo to you if he didn't believe you were the right person for it."

"Hmm," Avery said, picking up another fry and dunking it into her chocolate milk.

Elaine held back a grimace as Avery popped it into her mouth. "It's the same with God."

"What do you mean?"

"It's like 1 Corinthians 10:13. God doesn't give us anything that we cannot handle or overcome," Elaine explained.

"Oh yeah, I remember Pastor Mike talking about that verse a couple of weeks ago."

"Yes, that's right," Elaine said, nodding, proud of Avery for recalling the sermon. "The other thing to remember is that we can trust God to be with us and help us. God always wants the best for us, whatever that might be."

"So, when I'm having trouble getting over a tough part of the music, I should ask God for help?"

"I think that sounds like a great idea," Elaine said.

"What if I ask for help and then I ruin the solo anyway?"

Elaine stifled a giggle—not because it wasn't a good question, but because it was so unintentionally mature that it took her by surprise.

"I think in that case, you can ask God to help you learn from your mistakes, and use that new knowledge to do better the next time. That's what I try to do."

Avery smiled. "Makes sense." With that settled, she drained the last of her chocolate milk, then her eye caught something over Elaine's shoulder.

"What is it, hon?" Elaine asked.

"It's just the librarian—she's coming over to talk to you."

Elaine turned around to see Priscilla walking toward their table. She gave a little wave.

"Hi, Elaine," she said when she got close. "Avery, how's school?"

"Going good," Avery said in a friendly tone.

Priscilla looked very pretty in a kelly-green sweater and cream-colored skirt, her hair tied back in a pleasantly messy chignon.

"You look lovely today, Priscilla," Elaine said, then worried when the librarian blushed that she'd been too outgoing.

"Oh, thanks so much for saying."

Elaine smiled. She was happy to run into Priscilla but she got the feeling she wanted to say something more.

"It's so nice to see you here," Elaine said. "Are you having lunch?"

"Yes, I'm actually on a date with someone."

"Oh, how nice!" Elaine exclaimed.

"I saw you when I came in and I thought I'd stop by to give you a little update."

Elaine moved over in the booth and motioned for Priscilla to sit down at the table. "Yes, go on," she said.

"I'm sorry to say it, but I called the police yesterday to check in on the case before leaving work, and they don't have any new information."

Well, Elaine supposed, no news was better than bad news.

"Dan said the fingerprint test was inconclusive—there were only a few partials except Nathan's, of course, which is to be expected, and none of them matched any in the system."

"That's what I thought might happen, but I have to admit a part of me was hoping there would just be an easy match to some random criminal in the database."

Priscilla shook her head, frowning. "No, sorry. They said they've got a few new leads and possible motives to look into, but nothing they were willing to share with me yet. They said they were going to call Nathan and you on Monday, presumably to tell you the same information I just did."

Elaine had gotten stuck on Priscilla's words about the police finding new leads—probably the same ones she and Jan had discovered while watching *Treasure Travels* the morning before.

"All right, well, thanks for telling me, Priscilla. I really appreciate you passing on that information to me."

"No problem at all. I just want to know what happened to that statue, for Nathan and for the fund-raiser."

"I know," Elaine agreed. "Me too."

"I really wish I knew what to tell the board members when they call, which they've done a lot lately, and e-mail, and text." Priscilla rolled her eyes. "I know they're only concerned, but I can't relay what I don't know."

Elaine nodded. "I know you're concerned about having to cancel the event, but I really hope you'll consider giving it another few days or so. I still have faith that we can figure out what happened and get it back in time."

Priscilla's expression was doubtful, but she agreed to go ahead and wait a little while longer before making any firm decisions.

"Oh, and there's another thing," the librarian said, tapping a hand to her lap. "I don't know if it's anything significant, but it seemed like it might be something you'd want to know."

"I'm listening," Elaine said eagerly.

"You know that show on TV about the antiques dealers— the brothers—who go all over the New England area helping people figure out if their stuff is valuable or not?"

"Yes, yes, the Henderson brothers, Gary and Stuart. The show's called *Treasure Travels*."

"Yes, that's the one," Priscilla confirmed. "Well, anyway, I've heard they were in town, but you could have knocked me over with a feather when they showed up in the library the other day. I mean, it's not like they're George Clooney or something, but they are at least a little bit famous. It was weird seeing them standing there in my workplace. I know they're just people, but they're on TV, so it's kind of odd when you see them in real life."

Elaine couldn't believe what she was hearing. It seemed that the Hendersons certainly were keeping a very low profile, as Rose had suggested, because this was the first she'd heard of anyone setting eyes on the team.

"What were they doing in the library?" she asked, before realizing her question could be heard as mildly insulting. "I mean, I love the library, the whole town does, but what were those strangers specifically doing in there when they've got a show to film?"

"That's just it," Priscilla said. "The interesting part is that they were asking if I had any books or articles that might speak to the value of the Camden statue."

"And what did you tell them?" Elaine asked, on the edge of her seat now.

"I showed them a few articles on the microfiche—old ones from back when the statue was newly lost and people were speculating about what might have happened to it. Folks mostly lost interest over time, with the exception of a small group of scholars, none of whom seem to agree on its current whereabouts."

"Did you mention that Nathan might know how much it's worth?"

Priscilla shook her head. "No, I didn't. I thought about it, but I figured with the investigation going on, he's got enough to worry about without having those guys pestering him. They weren't exactly overly friendly," Priscilla said in a low voice, almost a whisper, "if you know what I mean."

"They were pushy?"

"Yes, that's exactly it. They seem so nice on television, like they just want to help people, but in real life—at least to me—they just seemed in a hurry to get an answer and go. They were disappointed when I didn't have anything more detailed to offer them, and they left without saying thank you or anything."

"That's a shame to hear," Elaine said, "and it certainly makes me rethink wanting to watch their program anymore."

"I feel the same way," Priscilla agreed. "Although I have to admit, I'll definitely catch the next episode since it has to do with the statue."

Elaine nodded. "I'm hoping it will reveal something as well, though I also plan to do what I can before then. Speaking of, did they happen to mention where they're staying while they're here in town? I don't think it could be Green Glade Cottages, or I'm sure Macy would have said something to me."

"They did mention it," Priscilla said. "Not to me, but I over-heard them talking about it with their producer while I was pulling up the microfiche. The whole lot of them are staying at the Corinth Hotel."

"Thanks, Priscilla," Elaine said. "That's really good to know."

Finally, she had something solid! She couldn't wait to get home and tell Jan so they could plan their next move.

CHAPTER TEN

Leaving Rose and Archie in charge of the tearoom, Jan and Elaine decided to take the next morning to do a little poking around. After their respective visits with Priscilla, the cousins had plenty to discuss as they settled into Jan's Camry for another trip to Waterville—to the Corinth Hotel, to be precise.

Jan wasn't sure exactly what they expected to find, but more often than not, she could count on a detail or two to pop out at her if she could see a place for herself. Of course they hoped that the Hendersons would be there, and even more of a stretch, they hoped to speak with the brothers and their guests, but if that wasn't possible, Jan and Elaine knew from experience that a few freshly baked treats could sometimes grease the wheels of people who might have seen or heard something.

Jan turned her key in the ignition and gave her twelve-year-old Toyota a chance to warm up. "So if the Hendersons were at the library recently asking about the value of the Camden statue, wouldn't you think they might have more than a strictly professional interest in it? Usually, the way the show works is that they have a guest on with something that may or may not be of value, and the whole point of the episode is to help that person figure it out. If it *does* have value, then they sometimes use their contacts to get it sold if the person doesn't plan on keeping it."

"Yes," Elaine said. "So, it doesn't make sense that they'd be personally invested in the Camden statue's price tag. It is possible that they've already gotten their hands on it, and are now researching its value before trying to sell it off."

"It is possible," Jan said, thinking, "but who would they sell it to? Everyone who is anyone in antique dealership around here is going to know that it's missing and probably stolen, whether they watch *Treasure Travels* or not."

"I agree," Elaine said, "on one caveat. There is always someone willing to buy something that's of value, even if it is illegal. There's a black market for stolen antiques, like there is for just about anything else you can think of."

"I don't like the sound of that," Jan said. "Though you're right."

"I don't either," Elaine added, "especially when I think about the implications of Nathan's involvement with the statue. And Harrison did say he'd been in the store recently to price some items." Elaine rubbed her eyes, looking stressed.

"Don't you think that Harrison would have said so if the thing Nathan asked about was the statue, after you told him it was missing?"

Elaine's mouth formed a thin line as she shook her head. "I don't know what to think when it comes to that man. He was evasive and strange when I asked him about it, and I'm not entirely certain he would have said anything even if he did know something about the statue."

"Well, evasive and strange pretty much describes Harrison all the time, doesn't it?" Jan asked, causing Elaine's frown to change into a grin.

"I can't argue with you there," Elaine said.

With the car adequately warmed up, Jan pulled out of the drive and made a right onto Main Street, headed for Waterville.

"Here we are," Elaine said, looking out her window as they pulled into the hotel parking lot several minutes later. The sky had cleared and there wasn't any snow in the forecast for that day, so it was a good time to get out and about.

"Do we have a plan?" Jan asked, cutting the ignition and unbuckling her seat belt.

"Not really. I think we'll just go in and see what happens. If they are filming *Treasure Travels*, surely those brothers can't be holed up in their room all day." Elaine glanced at her wristwatch. "It's breakfast time—maybe we'll catch them in the hotel café."

"Good point," Jan said. "I could go for a quick bite myself." The two had skipped their usual morning meal, wanting to get on the road.

The cousins got out of the car and Jan locked up. The building's main lobby was long and large, full of abstract art prints and several seating areas with sleek, industrial furniture. A gurgling, horizontal fountain separated the center of the lobby and was filled with colorful glass beads.

"I never noticed before," Elaine said, stopping briefly to look into the fountain, "that people seem use this as a wishing well."

Jan glanced in as well, then opened her purse and pulled out two pennies. "Have a go," she said, handing one to her cousin.

Elaine closed her eyes and then Jan did the same, but instead of making a wish, Jan said a little prayer. *Lord, please help us find something today that might help us figure out this case, so dear Elaine and Nathan can find peace. Amen.*

When Jan looked up, she saw Elaine open her eyes. The cousins shared a quick, knowing smile, and Jan guessed that her cousin had offered up a silent prayer as well.

With that, they wandered around the lobby for a few moments before heading to the desk. A pretty young woman with brown curly hair and olive skin asked if there was anything she could do to help them. Jan took a peek at her name tag, which identified her as Keira. "What a pretty name," she said.

The girl touched her tag. "Oh, thank you," she said, flashing a lovely smile.

"Would you mind directing us to the hotel restaurant?" Elaine asked.

"Of course," Keira said, coming out from behind the counter to join the two women. She pointed down a long corridor. "If you head down that hallway and take a right near that window close to the middle, it's just there."

"Thank you," Jan said. "Do they serve breakfast?"

"Yes, they do," Keira said, hurrying back behind the counter to reach under the desk. "Here are some menus so you can get a head start."

"Wonderful. Thanks again for your help," Elaine said, giving a little wave as they turned to follow the young woman's instructions.

"She was sweet," Jan said.

"Yes, she was," Elaine agreed. "And there are some pretty fabulous-looking dishes on this menu."

"And some pretty fabulous prices as well," Jan said.

"If by fabulous, you mean outlandish," Elaine said, causing them both to chuckle. "Maybe I'll just get a coffee and a croissant, though I'm sure it won't hold a candle to your maple ones."

Jan gave Elaine a playful nudge in the side with her elbow, just as they reached the restaurant. They were shown to a table next to a window and, as they ordered and nibbled on their breakfasts—Elaine's croissant and Jan's everything bagel with cream cheese—they admired the view of the river below.

Things were quiet for about twenty minutes, but then the two women heard a little commotion near the doorway. Turning their heads simultaneously, they saw what all the fuss was about. The few early-morning risers enjoying a quiet meal had all shifted in their seats and were murmuring about the group that had just entered the restaurant.

Stuart and Gary Henderson were there with a woman Jan recognized from their show's latest episode—Serina Frost—and all were surrounded by a camera crew holding a bunch of equipment. They were taken to an area not far from where Jan and Elaine sat, and Jan could tell from his arm movements that one of the camera guys was staking out the spot for good lighting.

"That's them," Elaine whispered. "What should we do?"

"Just keep doing what we're doing and finish our food. It looks like they're setting up to interview Serina. Maybe we can hear some of it from here," Jan said.

Elaine nodded. "Even if we can't, we can probably go up to them afterwards and say hello. It wouldn't be dishonest to say we're curious fans and want an autograph."

Jan grinned, nodding. "Good thinking. From what I've seen of Stuart, that sort of flattery can only help our cause."

They both went back to their food while trying to listen to the interview as best they could without getting noticed, but unfortunately the group was too far away. The only thing Jan could tell from where she sat was that Serina was none too happy to be talking to them on camera. When Stuart Henderson's questions concluded, Serina's features flooded with noticeable relief, and she scurried off to a table in a dark corner, as far from the crew as the small restaurant would allow.

Having finished their breakfast, Jan and Elaine looked at each other and nodded in silent agreement that it was time to go for it. Jan left money on the table to cover their meals and a tip, and they headed off toward the Hendersons, who didn't seem to be in a hurry to wrap up and leave the restaurant.

It was Gary who noticed them coming first, and Jan caught the flash of irritation that passed over his features before he rerouted them and fixed an unmistakably insincere smile on his lips. "Hello there, ladies," he greeted. "Is there something we can do for you?"

Hearing his brother, Stuart turned rapidly, and his was a very different reaction. Where Gary had looked put out at the sight of possible fans, Stuart was visibly ecstatic to have the attention. "Oh, good morning!" he sang out. "It's always wonderful to meet new fans. Would you like an autograph?"

Jan didn't miss it when Gary turned his face briefly to the side and rolled his eyes. As Priscilla had noticed, things weren't as sunny as they appeared on television, but then, that wasn't too surprising.

"Why, yes," Elaine said, reaching into her handbag for a pen, "if you don't mind, I'd love one."

Stuart clapped his hands together and then pulled a permanent marker out of his pocket. Jan couldn't help but grin at the realization he probably kept it there at all times, for situations such as their current one. Oh well, she supposed, everyone had their thing.

Jan and Elaine chatted with Stuart for a few minutes about how much they liked the show and what were their respective favorite episodes, then Jan expressed delight that *Treasure Travels* had come to Lancaster.

"We're staying here in Waterville," Gary corrected.

"Don't mind Gary," Stuart said, "we'll be making our way to Lancaster soon enough. How else are we going to get the best local gossip about who might have stolen it? Viewers love a good mystery."

Elaine spoke up. "Do you have any theories on what might have happened to it?" she asked casually.

Stuart scoffed. "To be honest, we aren't really interested in finding out. The longer it's missing, and the more scandal it causes, the better our situation."

Jan and Elaine glanced at each other. "Do you mean your...ratings?" Jan clarified hesitantly.

"Well, yeah," Stuart said.

Jan noticed Gary's face turning a shade of red. "That's enough, Stuart," he said between clenched teeth.

"Oh, come on," Stuart said, "everyone knows they've been low lately."

"Now they do," Gary seethed.

Jan could take a hint, and she sensed it was time to get out of there before their curiosity irritated Gary any further.

"Well, thanks so much for this," she said, holding up the napkin boasting Stuart Henderson's wavy signature.

"Oh, my pleasure," Stuart said, reaching out to shake her hand. "It's always nice to meet fans."

Elaine thanked the brothers too, and then they turned to leave. They were near the door when Jan noticed that Serina was no longer sitting at the table she'd chosen before.

"That was...interesting," Elaine whispered as they left the restaurant.

"No kidding," Jan said. "Now I know more about who the brothers are outside of the show than I ever wanted to, but at least we can probably rule them out as suspects."

"You think?" Elaine asked.

"You heard what Stuart said about their ratings being down—if their show is in jeopardy, they're probably after a good story, and finding the statue would absolutely be huge for their show."

"I'm not so sure," Elaine argued. "If the show fails, and they lose their jobs, they might be in need of a quick cash influx."

"*Hmm,*" Jan murmured. "I hadn't thought of that." They walked in silence for a moment. "Though, if they sold the statue, wouldn't their reputation as antiques experts be destroyed? Would they ever get work again if anyone found out?"

"That's a good point," Elaine sighed. "Initially I thought there weren't any plausible suspects, and now they're coming out of the woodwork." She stopped suddenly and gripped Jan's forearm. "Look," she said, pointing with her chin.

Jan followed her cousin's line of vision to a sign for a restroom just off the hallway. A woman stood underneath it, then disappeared inside.

"It's Serina," Elaine added.

"I wondered where she'd got to. I didn't see her in the restaurant when we left." Jan looked at Elaine. "I could stand to make a stop."

"All right," Elaine said. "While you do that, I'm going to go thank Keira for her help and ask if she's seen that other guest anywhere around here."

Jan nodded and went into the restroom. She was unsurprised to find that Serina had already gone into a stall, but she was surprised to discover that the woman had left her purse sitting on the sink. She decided instead to wash her hands, which were sticky from the little bit of cream cheese she'd gotten into. When she got to the sink, she had to move the handbag out of the way to turn the water on, and as she rinsed the soap from her fingers, Jan caught a flash of something metallic-looking out of the corner of her eye. She would not go so far as to look into another woman's purse, but when she went to pull a paper towel from the holder, she got a decent view inside. There, as clear as day, was a plaque, sticking up out of the bag, too big really to fit inside.

Jan's breath caught as she read the lettering.

CHAPTER ELEVEN

She couldn't see all of the words clearly, but Jan had caught a few—*Camden*, and *esteemed author*, along with some dates— and the overall image they formed was unmistakable.

It was the very plaque that adorned the Camden statue. Jan remembered its description clearly from skimming through Watkins's book.

But she didn't have too long to think about it because she heard a stall door creak, and did her best to remain calm while exiting the bathroom.

Catching sight of Elaine and Keira down the hallway, she hurried toward her cousin, arriving just in time to hear Elaine thank the concierge.

"Anything interesting?" Jan asked softly when they'd gotten their distance from Keira—she was about to burst with the knowledge of what she'd just seen.

Elaine nodded. "Keira was more open with me than I expected, so that's good. She said that Dr. Watkins is in fact staying here too. And here is the interesting part: he was initially supposed to appear on air along with Serina, but the concierge said there was a big falling out the other day, and Watkins threatened not to do the interview."

Jan's eyes widened.

Elaine spoke in a whisper. "Not only that, but he has a laptop and a notebook that he carries everywhere in a briefcase, and Keira said he's gotten really protective of it. He dropped it in the lobby the other day by mistake and nearly had a fit when she tried to pick it up and give it back to him."

"That is interesting," Jan said. "Oh, before I forget, did you give her the cookies we brought?"

"Sure did," Elaine answered. "That's not all, though. I thought that what we saw in the restaurant was the entirety of Serina's interview, but it seems they're not finished yet."

"What do you mean?" Jan asked as they shuffled through the hotel's revolving door and started for her car.

"The rest is going to be at Kate's Diner, tomorrow at lunchtime," Elaine said.

Jan unlocked the Camry and they got in. "Looks like we have lunch plans for tomorrow. And I haven't even told you what I found out in the bathroom."

Elaine looked at her expectantly as she pulled her seat belt over her lap and snapped it in place.

"I think Serina Frost has the plaque that belongs on the statue," Jan revealed.

"You're kidding," Elaine said. When Jan shook her head no, Elaine's mouth opened wide. "How do you know?"

"Her purse was sitting open on the counter when I went into the bathroom, and the plaque was sticking right up out of it," Jan said, still not fully believing what she'd seen.

"You're sure it was the same one from the statue?" Elaine asked skeptically.

Jan nodded. "No, I'm not absolutely certain," she said. "But it sure looks like it from the old picture in Watkins's book, and why would there be a copy? I don't know why Serina left her purse there or, more importantly, how she got her hands on that plaque in the first place, but I know what I saw."

Elaine was quiet for a moment. "Maybe she's so distraught from her father's recent death that she's not thinking clearly."

"Could be," Jan agreed. "Or maybe she's so distraught from her father's death, and the fact that he willed his most valuable possession to Lancaster, that she was motivated to take it. It would take some careful arrangement," Jan added. "That statue is way too big for a single grown man without a cart to move it, let alone a woman as small as Ms. Frost."

"I think the same would be true for whoever moved it, don't you?" Elaine asked.

"Yes," Jan said, turning on the car and then pulling out of the parking lot. "But maybe hired movers were used, unless the thief was just extraordinarily strong."

She watched the road ahead of her, pleased at the little bit of sunshine flooding through the window and warming her arm.

"About that lunch tomorrow," Jan continued. "You go and I'll handle the tearoom with Rose."

Elaine must have seemed unsure because Jan added, "Take Nathan with you. You'll get a chance to catch up, and it'll be fun. Maybe you can find out more about Serina and why on earth she has that plaque."

"I can think of one reason," Elaine said, voicing both their thoughts. "If she took the statue, and it fell off, she doesn't want anyone to find it and pin the theft on her. She probably thought it would be safe in her purse."

"Sounds like we've got our work cut out for us," Jan said as they began the drive back to Lancaster.

"It sure does," Elaine agreed.

THERE WAS A knock on the kitchen door of Tea for Two later that evening.

"I'll get it," Elaine called across the hall to the craft room, where Jan was busy working on her latest sewing project.

Elaine trundled down the stairs as fast as she could, and when she got to the door and opened it, she was pleased to find Nathan standing on the other side.

"Well, hi there," she said, walking into his outstretched arms. They embraced for a moment and then he pulled away. Elaine tried not to feel hurt at the brevity.

"Hey," he said. "How are you?"

"I'm doing okay," she answered, putting her hands into her pockets. "Come on inside and we'll talk."

Nathan hesitated. "No, thank you. I just stopped by because I miss you and wanted to see you for a minute to tell you that Dan called and said the police have a few leads they're looking into, but they weren't willing to share anything at this time. I can't stay though; I've got to run."

Elaine was unable to hide the confusion in her expression and Nathan looked pained.

"Okay," she said. "Where are you going?"

Something Elaine couldn't read passed over his features. "Business," he said. "But I promise I'll see you soon, and we'll have a chance to talk." He reached out and grasped her hand. "I know things are difficult right now because of the theft, but trust me when I say I'm not involved, and things will be all right once they catch the criminal who did this."

Elaine nodded sadly. "I do trust you, Nathan."

They were silent for a moment, watching as Earl Grey gingerly made his way across the snowy yard, then crouched down low as though he was hunting something.

"I'm going to Kate's tomorrow for lunch," she said, the hopefulness in her voice clear even to her own ears. "Would you like to come with me, or meet me there?"

Nathan shook his head. "No, sweetheart, I'm sorry. I can't make it."

"Oh," Elaine said, not bothering to hide the fact that he'd let her down.

"I'm sorry, I really am," he said, squeezing her hand. "How about next week I take you to dinner instead?"

"Yeah?" she asked, cheering just a little.

"Yeah. The job I'm working on will be finished then and we'll go out someplace nice. How does that sound?" he asked, searching her face.

The fatigue and strain in his voice was unmistakable, but he was trying to make her happy anyway. Her heart softened a little toward him.

"That sounds good."

The skin at the corners of his eyes wrinkled as he smiled. "Wonderful," he said, bending to kiss her cheek. "I'll call you before then and we'll sort out the details." He gave her a wan smile. "You pick the place."

"It's a date," she said, and he turned to go, leaving her thinking that, though he'd stopped by to talk to her, she had more questions now than answers.

THE NEXT MORNING when Elaine told Jan that Nathan wasn't going to be able to make it to lunch with her, Jan offered to come along instead. Rose and Archie assured the cousins that they had everything under control at Tea for Two.

"Are you sure?" Jan asked as she and Elaine bundled up, but Archie just clicked his tongue.

"Yes, yes, we're sure. We've got this, don't we, Rose?" Archie asked.

Rose winked at Jan and Elaine. "Absolutely."

"If you need anything, or it gets too busy and you want us to come back, give us a call," Elaine urged.

"We will," Rose promised, and then they were on the road to Kate's. The weather wasn't bad, so they'd decided to walk.

"I'll have eaten at Kate's twice this week," Elaine said. "She'll probably start to wonder what's wrong with the pastries at Tea for Two."

Jan laughed. "Well, we don't serve traditional meals, so I think she'll understand."

"If I keep eating her food, though," Elaine said, "my waistline won't understand."

"The walk will help," Jan encouraged, winking. "I should know." She'd gained a little weight a while back, but had since lost it, so she knew how Elaine felt.

"Oh sure, walking the few hundred yards to Kate's should burn off approximately one french fry."

The two women burst into laughter and strolled on companionably. When they got to Kate's, they both noticed that things looked even busier than usual, and there was a small crowd gathered just inside the door.

It didn't take long to figure out that Keira had been correct. Elaine spotted Stuart and Gary Henderson sitting across from Serina Frost at a booth, and the woman looked just about as happy as she had in the restaurant at the Corinth the day before.

"Shall we go ahead and try for a table?" Jan asked.

"Yes, let's," Elaine answered. "And then we can figure out how to get her to talk to us."

"That will be easier said than done," Jan said. "She doesn't look like she wants to talk to anyone."

"She did just lose her father," Elaine gently reminded her cousin as they slid into a booth as near to the commotion as they could find.

While the second part of Serina's interview took place, Elaine and Jan sipped sodas. Finally, it looked to be concluding, as the crew shut off the cameras and began to drift outside. The Hendersons shook Serina's hand and Elaine saw Gary pass her an envelope. She saw Jan watching as well.

"Do you think they paid her to do the interview?" Jan whispered. "Do they pay their guests?"

Elaine nodded. "I don't know. But there could be any number of things in that envelope."

The cousins watched as Stuart and Gary left through the front door, followed by a crowd of onlookers, some of whom were locals Elaine recognized, and some visitors who must have somehow heard about the show being in town.

Serina got up and reached under the table to retrieve a small suitcase.

Elaine had a sudden idea. "Hi there!" she called over the back of the booth.

Serina looked surprised but smiled and returned the greeting. "Hello."

"My name is Elaine and this is my cousin, Jan."

"Hi, I'm Serina," the woman said, reaching out a hand as she came near their table. "Is there something I can help you with?"

Since she was closer, Elaine noticed pale-purple thumb-print-shaped shadows beneath Serina's eyes. She looked at her cousin, whose eyes had widened as if to ask what Elaine was doing.

"Yes, there is," she said. "Why don't you sit down here and I'll buy you lunch."

Serina looked puzzled and a little suspicious, but maybe she was also just tired and hungry, because she agreed and sat down. "Okay. I guess that would be all right."

The young woman ordered from the menu and opened up a little as she chatted with Elaine and Jan. Finally, Elaine thought it best to cut to the chase. There wasn't much time before the library fund-raiser arrived. Priscilla was on the line as well as Nathan, and Elaine wanted to help them both. Perhaps that's where her bravery—or was it audacity—came from in that moment.

"This may sound odd," she started, "but my cousin was in the bathroom at the Corinth Hotel yesterday, washing her hands, and she happened to see something very unusual poking out of your purse."

Serina shot up straight in her seat. "You—you what? You looked in my purse? I don't even know you!"

Jan held out a hand. "I'm really sorry. I was washing my hands in the bathroom, as Elaine said, and your purse was there, on the counter. I assure you I didn't touch the plaque."

Serina wasn't quite placated, but she did look a little embarrassed. "Oh my goodness. You're right. I did leave it on the counter, didn't I?"

Jan nodded, smiling softly. "Yes, and it wasn't my intention to see in it, but I had to move it to get to the sink, you understand?"

Serina nodded. "I guess that makes sense. Maybe instead of being mad, I should be thanking you for not stealing it."

"On the contrary," Jan said. "I should be apologizing. I should have called out to you when I saw it, and told you that you'd left it there."

Serina released a big breath of air. "It's all right. It really is. My head just isn't where it should be lately." She took a sip of her water. "You see, my father died, and, well, we weren't close, but I do miss him. Ever since the funeral, I haven't been thinking straight."

The words started pouring from the young woman and Elaine's heart went out to her. She must not have talked to anyone about her grief until then.

"Even though we didn't get along that well, especially as he got older and more reclusive, I still loved him. It broke my heart when he left that statue to a town I've never even heard of."

Elaine and Jan exchanged a glance.

"Do you mind if I ask how you ended up with the plaque?" Elaine asked.

A range of emotions passed over Serina's delicate features, and her dark eyes looked cloudy behind her glasses. "I...I found it, the other night, down by the docks."

"You found it?" Jan asked, and Elaine was certain Serina heard the skepticism in her voice.

"I know it sounds weird, but it's true."

The cousins both nodded.

"I was taking a walk down by the shore, to clear my head. This *Treasure Travels* show has really been stressing me out—all the questions they ask that I don't have answers to. They keep assuming I knew my father's last living years far better than I actually did."

Elaine gave her an encouraging smile and she went on.

"Anyway, I agreed to the interview because they said they'd pay me. I think they thought I might know where the statue is and was keeping it a secret, but I don't—honest. I just needed the money."

"Are you in trouble?"

Serina shook her head. "No, not in trouble exactly. I just...well, I lost my job recently, and I haven't been able to find a new one, so money's tight."

"I can imagine that when your father died and didn't leave his most valuable possession to you, it upset you," Jan prodded softly.

"*Mmm-hmm,*" Serina said. "I'm his only living relative, so it hurt my feelings and, I hate to say this, but it made me angry too."

"It's understandable that you'd have those feelings," Elaine said.

Serina took another sip of water. "I know I have to turn in the plaque," she said, sounding guilty but also sad and resigned. "I just knew that the police would take it in as evidence and maybe even think I stole the statue, but all I wanted was to hang on to it for sentimental value. It just seemed like fate when I found it down at the docks—like my dad had left me a piece of himself after all."

Elaine's heart gave a little tug as the truth and candor of Serina's statement sank in. This girl wasn't guilty. She was a heartbroken orphan wondering why her father had rejected her.

"My dad was a strange person," Serina went on. "He had a hard time showing his feelings, and for most of my life, he seemed more interested in his collections than he was in me or my mom. That's probably why they split when I was young. I didn't see him much over the years, and I regret not having a better relationship with him, but I still feel disappointed when I think about the fact that an author he never met held more interest to my father than his own kid did. And those two from the show—the Hendersons—are the same way. They only care about how much money the statue is worth. That's practically all they asked me about."

Elaine caught Jan's eye and saw that her cousin didn't miss the implication of Serina's comment.

"I'm so sorry you've been through so much trouble," Jan said.

"I'll be okay," Serina said. "I've got the check from the interview and I got a call this afternoon for an interview in Augusta."

Elaine smiled. "That's wonderful. We'll keep you in our prayers and ask that, if it's the right job for you, God will show you favor."

Serina looked surprised but pleased. "Thanks," she said, "that means a lot."

Jan and Elaine both nodded and they continued to chat for a while longer with Serina as she finished her lunch. Looking a little less weary than when she'd arrived at their table, Serina finally gathered her bags, said goodbye, and headed for the door.

"She's a sweet woman after all," Jan said.

Elaine fiddled with her napkin. "Yes, she is," she said with a sigh.

"I know. That doesn't really help." Jan's forehead creased in concern.

"It does and it doesn't," Elaine said. "On the one hand, I don't really know what to do next. On the other, I want to believe her story."

Jan nodded as the check came. "I do too."

"All the same," Elaine said, "I think we should ask Dan if she turned in that plaque, the next time we see him."

"That would be wise. After all, sometimes people say whatever they can to look innocent."

CHAPTER TWELVE

They didn't have to wait long to speak to Trooper Benson since he stopped by the tearoom the next morning.

"Hi there, Dan," Jan greeted as she approached a table by the fire where Rose had seated him.

"Good morning, Jan," he said politely.

"Can I get you some tea or something to eat?" Jan asked, feeling out whether he was there for breakfast or for business.

"Yes, that would be great. How about a cup from your not-so-secret coffee stash, and maybe one of those maple croissants that are so good?"

"Coming right up," she said.

On the way back to the kitchen, she checked on a few tables. Macy Atherton was there with her daughter-in-law, Zale, and fielding her questions about the missing statue was becoming more and more challenging as the morning went on.

"Oh, Jan, there you are," Macy said as Jan approached her table. "I was wondering when you'd be back around. Thought you might have gone missing like that statue."

Jan smiled with ease—she was used to the prickly woman. Macy might have a rough exterior, but Jan knew from experience that her insides were made of gold, or at least, gold plated. There were plenty of times Macy had shown kindness, not the least of which was in the number of visitors she referred to the tearoom when they came to stay at Green Glade, the cottages she ran with her son and his wife. She might make it difficult for people to get to know her, but they always learned that if they stuck with her long enough, it was worth it.

"I'm right here," Jan said, letting the comment roll off her shoulders. "It's a busy morning."

"That I can see. This place gets more and more crowded every day."

Zale and Jan exchanged a glance, knowing some of that was thanks to Macy herself.

"Can I get you anything else, or would you like your check?" Jan asked.

"The check will be fine," Macy said. "But can you also tell me whether or not there have been any breakthroughs regarding the statue, and if Priscilla will have to cancel the fund-raiser?"

Jan shook her head. "I'm afraid I don't know much more than you at this time."

Inadvertently, she cast a glance over at Dan Benson, and Macy saw.

"I'm sure Priscilla will keep the board posted as soon as she knows anything new," Jan said.

Macy's mouth formed a Cheshire cat grin. "All right," she said. "You have a good day now, Jan. Thanks for the breakfast."

"Yes, thank you," Zale added. "It was delicious as usual."

"And don't let that trooper leave hungry," Macy added.

Jan said a silent prayer for patience as she carried her tray back to the kitchen. Rose was on baking duty that morning, so she was serving, and she had to admit, she was a little jealous of their assistant at the moment.

"Elaine," she said when she got to the other side of the kitchen door, "fill in for me for a little while, would you?"

"Sure. Is everything okay?" Elaine asked, halfway done with filling up a tray.

"Oh yes, it's fine," Jan said, placing her own tray full of dirty dishes near the sink to manage when she returned. "It's just that Dan Benson is out there and I think he'd like to speak with me about the case."

"Well, go on then, by all means," Elaine said.

Jan nodded and filled a mug with some fresh coffee and plated a warm maple croissant.

When she got to Dan's table, he asked if she might sit for a moment. "I don't have much new information," he said, "so don't get too excited, but I would like to chat if you've got the time."

"Of course," Jan said, smoothing her apron as she took the seat across from him. The fire crackled in the hearth, and Jan was grateful for the brief chance to sit down.

"How are Charlotte and the kiddos?" Jan asked.

Dan smiled. "It's great to have Charlotte back," he said. "The kids are messy and exhausting, and wonderful as usual."

Jan chuckled. "That's family, isn't it?"

"It sure is," he said, spreading a big dollop of butter on his croissant. "It's a handful with the job and all, but I couldn't ask for anything better."

"Glad to hear it," Jan said, knowing exactly what he meant.

She watched as Dan quickly added a little sugar to his coffee and took a sip.

"So, I've got good news and bad news. Which do you want first?" He looked at her carefully.

"Let's start with the bad," Jan suggested. "That way, the good might have a shot at making up for it."

Dan grinned, then his face became serious as he turned on his law enforcement business manner. "Well, the bad news is that the fingerprint tests didn't turn up anything useful."

No surprise there, Jan thought. Elaine had concluded the same with her home test, finding nothing but partial prints.

"Good news is we've got a few new persons of interest." He studied his croissant. "As I'm sure you know, that antiques show is in town. I can't for the life of me remember the name, but—"

"*Treasure Travels*," Jan filled in.

"Yes, that's the one," he said, picking up the croissant. "Anyway, they're in town and have brought up a few questions, what with the timing of their arrival here coinciding with the theft of the statue. If you ask me, it's a little unusual to have so many folks who are interested in that artifact in the same place, right at the time it goes missing."

He glanced at Jan and she nodded in agreement.

"So, we're looking into that."

"Has anything come of it so far, that you can share with me?"

"Well, one of the people they were interviewing on the show turned up with a piece of evidence."

He didn't say so, but Jan knew he was most likely referring to the plaque that Serina Frost had found.

"The person said they found it down at the docks, but they turned it in voluntarily and, after investigating, we didn't find any reason not to let that person go."

"Okay," Jan said, not wanting to reveal that she knew the "person" was a she and that it was Serina. The local law enforcement was supportive and appreciative of the help Jan and her cousin often offered in solving mysteries, but she knew there was a thin line between helping and hindering, and she preferred to err on the side of caution when it came to getting involved with investigations.

Dan took another sip of coffee, then set the mug down. "I really hate to be the bearer of bad news, and we're not able to prove it yet, but if I had to guess, I'd say whoever stole that statue likely had it shipped off for sale, and it's probably gone for good."

"Oh no," Jan said. "Nathan will be devastated if it's been sold off to someone. That statue means so much to him, and to the library." She glanced up at Dan. "I hate to ask, but, is Nathan still a suspect?"

Dan nodded, his lips pursed. "Unfortunately, yes. And that's one of many reasons why we're working hard to figure out what really happened."

"We certainly appreciate all that you do."

"Just doing my job. And I don't want you all to give up just yet. It's just that I don't like people getting their hopes up only to be disappointed. I'd rather lay the possibilities out for you up front so you know what we could find."

"I understand," Jan said. "And I'll be happy to pass all of this on to Elaine."

"All right then," Dan said. "This breakfast was great, but I've got to get back to work now. Can you bring the check for me?"

"Oh, don't worry about it," Jan said. "It's on us today, as a thank-you for the update."

"That's nice of you," he said, rising from the table to shake her hand. "I'll keep you posted. In the meantime, take care of yourselves."

"We will, Dan," Jan promised.

She had just returned to the kitchen with Dan's breakfast things when Elaine waved wordlessly to get her attention.

"What is it?" Jan asked.

Elaine looked over at Rose, who was mixing up a batch of muffins, and motioned for Jan to join her in the pantry.

"Why are we hiding in here?" Jan asked, confused.

"I didn't want Rose to hear, but Clifton's out in the west parlor," Elaine said. "He's asking for you."

Jan put a hand on her chest. "Oh goodness," she said. "What do I do if he asks me out? I don't know what to say, probably because I don't completely know how I feel about the idea."

Elaine gave her a quick squeeze and smiled reassuringly. "We talked about this, remember? You'll be fine."

"I know, but I'm still not sure about it."

Elaine nodded. "I know what you mean, but this isn't a marriage proposal, and Bob is not here. Clifton's a nice, good man. Just like we talked about, it won't hurt anything to have lunch with him. Then, after that, you can see how you feel and what you want to do next."

"You're right," Jan said. "And I agree with you." She squared her shoulders. "Besides, we don't even know what he's going to ask until he asks it. He might just want stock tips or something, in which case, I'll be even less helpful than if he asks me out to lunch."

"You're just nervous," Elaine said. "But you have nothing to worry about. Listen to your heart and trust in what it tells you, and things will work out the way they're meant to."

"All right," Jan said. "Thank you."

"It's what I'm here for." Elaine winked.

Thankfully, Rose was too busy to notice the two silly women coming out of the pantry with nothing in their hands, and Jan headed off to find Clifton.

He was seated at the same table where he'd been the last time he'd stopped by to talk to her, and she tried not to read too much into that. He'd probably just picked a spot at random. She had almost convinced herself of that until she got closer to the table and Clifton's face lit up as if he was seeing sunshine for the first time in a decade. Jan's throat dried up. She didn't know if she could handle that kind of pressure. What if Clifton really did like her and she went out with him only to find that she couldn't reciprocate the feelings?

It was times like this that she missed Peter the most. Lengthy marriages developed a rhythm and a cadence that became comfortable over time. They weren't always exciting, but there was a beauty in their steady movement, like that of the passing seasons. She missed knowing what to do and say without thinking so much about it.

"Hello, Clifton," she greeted as she came up to his table.

"Good morning," he said, then stood and pulled out the chair across from him, gesturing for her to sit. "It's so nice to see you again."

"Same to you," Jan said. "Can I get you anything?"

"Actually, I'm just here to see you," he said, his cheeks turning the slightest shade of pink.

Jan had to admit it was charming, and she couldn't help but feel flattered by the attention.

"Oh?" Jan said in question.

"Yes. Jan, if it would be all right with you, I'd like to take you out to lunch sometime."

Jan felt her cheeks warming. The moment of truth had arrived, and yet she still hadn't made a firm decision. It was too late to think on it much now. If she didn't say anything soon, she would come across as rude, and that was the last thing she wanted. Knowing he had lost his wife, and knowing how hard it was to be a spouse adrift after such a loss, Jan understood that it had taken guts for Clifton to ask her at all. If she wasn't absolutely certain she did not want to get to know him better, she owed it to him to give it a chance.

She offered the man a warm smile, which he happily returned. "Yes, Clifton, that sounds very nice."

"Oh, that's good news," he said, sounding relieved. "I'll call you with the details in just a few days. Does that sound okay?"

"That sounds perfect," Jan said.

ELAINE AND ROSE were standing dangerously close to the door when Jan returned to the kitchen. It was a miracle she hadn't hit them when she came in.

"I hope you two are aware that you can't hear through this door and all the way across to the west parlor," Jan said, hands on her hips.

"We know," Rose said, giggling. "At least we do now."

Jan looked at Elaine incredulously. "Did you tell her about it?" she asked her cousin.

Elaine at least had the decency to look guilty. "I may have," she admitted, placing a hand over her mouth after the words escaped. "But Rose is okay with it, aren't you, Rose?"

Rose just shook her head and laughed. "Of course. I'm just excited that my dad is spending time with you. He wasn't doing so well there for a while, and it's nice to see him trying again."

Jan tilted her head. "Are you sure it doesn't bother you that your father asked your boss out to lunch?"

"I'm happy about it, actually," Rose said, giggling. "Besides, I've got my own dating life to worry about."

Jan was relieved at the change of subject. She hadn't meant to draw attention to herself, and, despite their good intentions, it was nice to switch to talking about Rose instead of herself.

"Speaking of," Elaine chimed in, "how did things go the other night with Emma's dinner?"

Rose's features glowed when she began to talk about her boyfriend and his little girl, and Jan could see that the young woman would make a wonderful mother someday.

"It was great," Rose said, pouring muffin batter into a tin lined with pale-blue paper cups. "But I guess I hadn't thought through the possible repercussions of letting such a young kiddo choose what to have for dinner."

"Oh my," Jan said. "Do I even want to ask?"

Rose and Elaine laughed.

"It wasn't that bad," Rose said. "It just wasn't the most balanced meal you'd imagine."

"No doubt," Elaine said. "Did she choose cake as the main course?"

"Close enough," Rose answered. "Pancakes."

"Now, that doesn't sound so bad," Jan said, waving a hand. She went to the oven to open it for Rose so she could put the muffins in to bake.

"That was just the beginning though," Rose said, pulling a face. "The side dish was frosted cereal, followed by a dessert of pink frosted cupcakes."

Elaine and Jan shared a glance, then burst out laughing.

"I'm surprised I didn't end up frosted myself by the end of it. I was so full of starchy carbs I could barely make it out of the car when Brent dropped me off at home."

By the time Rose finished with her story, they were all giggling.

Jan and Elaine finished up at four o'clock, and then decided to share a supper of ravioli and a Caesar salad. By the time they headed upstairs to watch the news and spend a quiet evening in their sitting room, Jan was feeling much better. As she worked on a dress she was making for Kelly, she thought at first of how much she missed Bob, and then of how many blessings she had in her life. A beautiful home, wonderful family and friends, a job she adored, and even her sewing, a hobby that fulfilled her creative side almost as much as baking but in a different way, and that allowed her to make things for those she loved.

It was a good life. And, as usual, counting her blessings made it that much easier to bear the things she missed. If she was honest about it, there was a blank space in her heart that she'd once thought was only open for Bob. But now, she wasn't so sure. She wasn't ready to let him go—she loved him and if he came back to Lancaster, she would be thrilled—but she also deserved to live a little, and saying yes to Clifton had made her feel confident and lively.

Elaine had been right—she'd followed her heart and it had led her to say yes. The only thing bothering her now was that she didn't know what her heart was going to say next, or if she would be ready when it did.

CHAPTER THIRTEEN

D o you think she's ready?" Jan asked as she helped Elaine with a necklace clasp. They were getting ready for a preliminary rehearsal of Avery's concert that evening and had both admitted that they were starting to feel nervous, as though they themselves had to play the music. The cousins had laughed at the silliness of that notion, but Elaine was praying for the girl all the same, especially after their conversation at Kate's the other day.

She knew how important this was to Avery, and she wanted to be there to support her young friend, whether she did well or not. The more family and friends Avery had around, encouraging her, the more she would understand that they all loved her no matter how she played.

"I think she's as ready as she can be," Elaine answered, catching Jan's eye in the mirror as her cousin struggled with the clasp Elaine hadn't been able to fasten on her own. It really was a tricky one, but she loved that particular piece of jewelry, and its aqua stones went so well with the greenish-blue sweater dress she'd chosen for the night and paired with short navy heels. It wasn't the world's most practical outfit for a winter night, but she'd been waiting for a chance to wear it, and, with her heavy coat, it would do just fine.

"She's been practicing so hard, and I know she's confident in her ability to get through the music well," Elaine said. "It'll just be a matter of her getting her bearings and doing her best to ignore the crowd so she can concentrate on the notes."

"There," Jan said, "I finally got it."

"Thank you," Elaine said, reaching up to run her fingers along the smooth beads. "I don't know why I go to the trouble with this thing, but I like it. You don't think it's too formal for a rehearsal?"

"No, I think it's pretty," Jan said. "I'm wearing this nice dress as well. I think it will be good to make the kids feel like this evening is as close to the real thing as possible. Audience clothes included." She checked the clasp on Elaine's necklace one last time and admired her cousin's reflection in the mirror before heading across the hall to grab her purse from her own room.

A few moments later, they were ready to go. Taking Elaine's car, they drove out of town into Augusta, arriving at Truman Middle, Avery's school, a few minutes early. Jan had asked if Elaine wanted to say hello to Avery before the event began, but Elaine was adamant that it would only increase Avery's anxiety about being onstage and ultimately, Jan had agreed.

The music hall was fairly crowded for a rehearsal, and Elaine was happy to see such a turnout. It would be great for Avery's orchestra to have a large group to practice in front of in preparation for the big night.

She and Jan stopped at the refreshments table someone had set up near the back, each taking a warm apple cider and a sugar cookie. They found seats and greeted the other students' family members around them, then quietly nibbled on their treats until the lights flickered twice and dimmed.

Elaine said a little prayer for Avery's confidence in the work she'd put into practicing, and for her to do well so she could see that God had taken care to honor her devotion to her music. Finally, she saw the students filing in to their chairs in the soft light, and she spotted Avery, nudging Jan to make sure she'd been able to pinpoint her granddaughter among the other kids. Elaine's stomach fluttered with butterflies as they listened to several lovely pieces, leading up to Avery's solo. When it was finally time, she caught herself leaning forward in her seat to better hear, and also partly because of nerves.

As Avery began to play, Elaine felt some of her anxiety dissipate. The child was doing so well! All that worry Avery had been feeling had been for nothing after all.

But then, several measures in, something happened. Avery missed only one note, as far as Elaine could tell, but that single note seemed to throw her off completely. It was as if all it took to knock down her sails was one tiny little breath of wind. And it only got worse from there.

Elaine's heart sank and she could feel Jan's joy deflating next to her. Oh, Avery would be so disappointed in herself, even though she needn't be.

Finally, she played the last few notes of her solo piece. Elaine was thankful for the low light—she knew Avery's face would be the same color as an apple, and she was glad for small mercies.

She and Jan exchanged a sad glance and then settled back into their seats to listen to the rest of the concert, their hearts not really in it anymore.

Elaine was ruminating on how hard it would be on Avery when she caught herself focusing on the negative. She took what she'd been thinking and worked quickly to turn it around, preparing to be as encouraging as possible for Avery.

When the music ended, the audience applauded loudly, and then, as the lights came back up and the clapping subsided, all of the students stood from their chairs and made their way to the back of the stage.

"That didn't go so well," Jan said, frowning as she picked up her handbag from under her seat. "Her little heart's going to be broken."

"I know," Elaine said. "It will. But she's a strong girl, and we need to be even stronger for her. Eventually she'll be fine if she knows she has a safe place to land."

Jan nodded.

The two women said goodbye to the parents they'd met around their seats and headed to the back of the stage to meet Avery and Kelly, and Brian and Paula, who had helped set up the event with a few of the other parents. Elaine spotted Avery in one of the chairs, her slim shoulders hunched over as Paula gently rubbed her back.

She and Jan exchanged a glance as they approached.

"Hi," Elaine said, checking Paula's and Brian's expressions for clues as to how to proceed. It was difficult to know what to say. She didn't want to make Avery feel worse about her performance than she already did, but not to acknowledge that it hadn't gone well would ring false and would be even more upsetting.

Paula gave a little nod and Brian smiled sadly when they heard Elaine's greeting, and she motioned for her and Jan to sit in the chairs alongside Avery.

After a few seconds of tense silence, Elaine spoke. "It didn't go the way you wanted it to, did it?"

Avery shook her head slowly, but when she looked up, Elaine was pleased to see there was no trace of tears in her eyes. "It was a disaster," Avery said.

The distraught tone in the child's voice, as if it was the worst day of her life—and perhaps being as young as she was, it was indeed—made Elaine want to chuckle a bit, but she knew the time wasn't right. One day Avery would reach a point where she could laugh at this, and see it for the learning experience it truly was, but that day hadn't yet come. There would be plenty more heartbreak in the young girl's life, as there was in most, but the way she handled this would set the tone for the rest, and Elaine was glad to see she hadn't given in to the urge to cry.

"That may be," Jan said, patting the girl on her leg, "but the good thing is, it's over."

Avery didn't respond.

"And now you know what to do differently next time," Elaine added. Paula smiled. "That's what a rehearsal is for."

Avery lifted her head a little and seemed to consider the words. "I guess that's true. There was a part where I slipped up, and"—she held up a palm—"I couldn't seem to get control of the music again. When I lost that beat, I sort of froze."

"There you go," Elaine continued. "You know exactly what part made you lose your concentration, so when you practice, you can focus on that place in particular and maybe work on getting through it more smoothly."

Avery nodded. "Thanks. It's good advice. I think I will try that." With that, she lifted her shoulders and sat back in the chair, glancing at the people around her. "Even though I was awful, I'm really glad you came."

They all grinned. "We are too, honey," Brian said. "We wouldn't have missed it for anything."

"I just hope I can give you a better show next time, at the real deal."

Elaine laughed. "I'm sure you will," she said.

She and Jan spent a few more minutes chatting with Avery and her mother, and then they parted ways so Paula and Brian could take Avery and Kelly for a burger on the way home.

On their way back through the auditorium to leave, Elaine spotted Katelyn Conrad waving at her from across the room. Jan went to say hello to a friend from church and the two agreed to meet back at the car.

"Hi, Katelyn," Elaine said as the young woman from the library board met her in the middle of the room. "What brought you here tonight?"

"Hey there, Elaine. I'm just helping Frank."

"Oh, that's right," Elaine said. She should have guessed. Frank Conrad, Katelyn's husband, was a music teacher and orchestra and band instructor at Avery's school.

"Did you come to watch Avery play?" Katelyn asked, graciously giving away nothing in her expression about the girl's performance.

"I did. She's doing okay, I think, or at least she will be. That kid has been practicing so hard and what happened tonight was tough on her."

Katelyn nodded sympathetically. "These students put so much pressure on themselves these days, they don't leave any room for the parents to do it for them."

Elaine smiled at the gentle joke. "I know what you mean. She really wanted to do well. I think the best we can do now is to show her that she doesn't have anything to prove—her family and friends will love her no matter what."

"That's exactly right," Katelyn agreed.

The two women visited for a few more minutes, and then Katelyn's expression turned serious.

"Listen, have you heard anything else about the missing statue?" Katelyn asked hesitantly.

Elaine got the feeling the young woman might think she was stepping on toes, since Nathan and Elaine were dating.

"I have heard a few things, and I've been in touch with Trooper Benson."

Katelyn looked hopeful and Elaine regretted that she would be the one to dash that.

"But they don't have anything concrete yet," Elaine added.

"Have they made any arrests that you know of?" Katelyn crossed her arms.

Elaine shook her head. "No, not that I know of. They do have a few leads they're exploring though, so don't give up hope just yet."

Katelyn nodded. "I'm sure I'm not the first board member to ask you about it, am I?"

"Not me directly," Elaine said. "But Macy's come into the tearoom and spoken to Jan about it."

Katelyn's eyes widened. "I'm sure that wasn't an easy conversation."

"No," Elaine confirmed. "I don't suppose it was."

"Do you think Priscilla will decide to cancel the fund-raiser?" Katelyn asked, wringing her hands.

"To be honest," Elaine answered, "I don't know. But I don't think she should yet, and I've expressed as much to her. There are still a few days to find out what happened, and Jan and I are looking into things ourselves. It may be a long shot, but I still believe it will be recovered, and that things will work out all right."

Katelyn looked skeptical but nodded anyway. "Thank you for talking with me about it. The board has been awfully quiet and I don't think that's helping anyone feel better about the situation."

"No," Elaine said, "I can't imagine it would. And you're welcome to ask me about it anytime, but I do promise to keep in touch with Priscilla the second I know anything."

Elaine thanked Katelyn and complimented her help on making the rehearsal comfortable and successful, and pulled on her coat before heading out to the car to meet Jan. She hoped her cousin hadn't been waiting too long since Elaine had the keys, but she was glad to see Jan exiting the building at nearly the same time as she was.

"Let's get that car of yours started," Jan said, feigning a shiver. "It is too cold for comfort out here."

"Even for a lifelong Mainer like yourself?" Elaine teased. "I'm surprised to hear you say so."

"Oh, stop it," Jan said, swatting Elaine playfully on the arm.

They drove home quietly, both feeling tired from the day and thinking about Avery's difficult night. After they'd changed into more comfortable clothes and settled in back at the house, Elaine found Jan working in her sewing room.

"May I come in?" she asked, knocking softly on the door.

"Of course," Jan said, looking up from her sewing.

"That looks complicated," Elaine said, squinting at the elaborate pattern near Jan's work.

"Oh, this? No, it's not so bad. It just takes some practice and some lessons best learned by making mistakes," Jan said, setting one last stitch by hand.

"Just like Avery," Elaine said.

"Yes, just like." Jan put the sewing down.

"I don't know how you manage to be so good at both baking and sewing," Elaine said.

"I think I've gotten good at them because I enjoy them. It doesn't feel like work to make something pretty or especially tasty."

Elaine was still standing in the doorway with folded arms when Jan waved her in.

"Come, sit down," Jan said.

"I don't want to bother you," Elaine argued, but Jan just waved that idea away.

"You're not bothering me at all," Jan reassured her. "This doesn't have a deadline—I just thought, since we've been spending so much time with Avery lately, that I'd make Kelly a little Sunday dress."

"I love the daisy pattern," Elaine said, studying the fabric laid out on Jan's sewing table. "Is it for spring?"

"Yes, that's what I'm hoping. Helps me get through the long winter, anyway, looking at the flowers while I work."

"I like that idea," Elaine said. "Thinking along those lines, I've been wondering if there's something I can get for Avery, to weather the season, so to speak."

Jan looked up. "Like what?"

"I don't know," Elaine said. "I haven't thought too much about it yet. But I was sort of thinking along the lines of a book—maybe some encouraging scripture having to do with pulling through a tough time. I know tonight was just a rehearsal, but Avery's struggling with confidence, and I'd like to give her something helpful."

"That sounds nice," Jan said. "I think she would really like that, and it would be something she could hold on to and refer to at different times in her life, even past what she's currently going through."

"Yes," Elaine said, nodding. "That's exactly what I was thinking."

"Why don't we go over to the Bookworm tomorrow and see if we can find the right thing?" Jan suggested.

"That sounds perfect," Elaine said, then decided to change the subject. "So, have you decided on a place you want Clifton to take you for lunch?"

"You and Rose," Jan said, shaking her head, but smiling all the same. "I can't even think for the two of you asking me for updates all the time."

"We're just curious. We're both settled in our own relationships, so we need to live vicariously through yours to experience that newness again," Elaine teased.

"I'd trade the newness for the oldness any day," Jan said, rolling her eyes. "I don't like the way this feels— beginning something new with someone new."

"It's just lunch," Elaine said. "Just keep reminding yourself that there's no pressure. He just wants to get to know you. It might turn out that he doesn't even like you at all."

Jan reached over and gently punched Elaine in the shoulder.

"I'm just trying to get you to laugh. Don't take it so seriously," Elaine said. "Just pick a place you think sounds like fun and let the guy treat you to a nice meal."

"You make it sound so easy," Jan said.

Elaine grew serious. "I know it's not so easy." She was thinking of Nathan as well and how long it had taken her to be ready to date him. "But it is worth it. The very worst thing that could happen is that you decide you don't want to have lunch with Clifton Young again, and then you won't ever have to think about it at all."

Jan giggled. "If only Avery and I had your confidence."

Elaine smiled humbly, appreciating the compliment, but deep in her heart, she was feeling anything but confident that night. Trying to be strong for both Nathan and Avery was taking its toll, and she needed to draw strength from somewhere so that she could continue to give it out to those she loved.

And she only knew one place to gather that strength. Elaine said good night to her cousin and went back to her room, where she quietly turned to God, the strongest of all.

CHAPTER FOURTEEN

Not that she was partial, but the Bookworm bookstore was one of Jan's favorite places in Lancaster. And for good reason. Bristol Payson was one of the friendliest people you could ever meet, who happily went out of her way to do extra special things for her customers, such as carrying the puzzle magazine *Cryptograms* just for Jan.

Elaine had asked if she wanted to come along while she shopped for a little book of verses for Avery, and Jan happily agreed. The sky was shining with a rare break from the usually heavy snow clouds, and the bookshop looked adorable even in the winter. During the summer months, Bristol kept outdoor furniture on her front lawn and often served lemonade to customers who liked to hang around reading the latest best seller, but the lounge chairs had been stowed away in the fall.

Given the Bookworm's cozy proximity to Tea for Two, Jan and Elaine opted to walk over, despite the frigid temperatures. Their breath revealed itself in small puffs of steam as they made their way to the charming shop. They passed through the little front gate, hurried inside the door of the pretty, shingled Cape Cod, and were greeted by warmth and the scent of coffee and hot chocolate.

The little bell above the shop door jangled and Bristol hollered "hello" from somewhere in the back. Jan and Elaine shouted return greetings and began to browse.

Elaine headed off into the blond wood shelves to a section of spiritual books and Jan perused a table arranged with newly released hardbacks. Each shiny, inviting book had a handwritten note about why a staff member liked it, and Jan let herself get drawn into the descriptions until she heard someone approach her from behind.

"That one was so good," Bristol said, and Jan turned to smile at the shop owner.

Her blonde hair was down around her shoulders and she wore jeans and a poppy-colored sweater over a plaid shirt of various reds and blues. Jan thought the clothes were a lovely reflection of the cheerful woman within.

"Hey there, Bristol. So, you liked this one, huh?" Jan asked, holding up the fat new book she'd picked up.

"Oh yeah. I love a good mystery, and that one was no disappointment. I can't say much, though, or I'll ruin it for you." Bristol winked.

"I think I'll take it then," Jan said. "I've been meaning to read more lately."

"Good choice. Is there anything special you're looking for that I can help with?" Bristol asked, hooking her fingers in the belt loops of her pants.

"Not me, no, but I think Elaine maybe could use some advice," Jan said, pointing to where her cousin stood staring at a shelf, her forehead creased.

"Ah, I see her," Bristol said before heading in Elaine's direction. "I've got the latest issue of that puzzle magazine you like," she called over her shoulder. "Don't let me forget to grab it for you when you check out."

"I won't," Jan assured her. She finished looking at the table and went over to join Elaine and Bristol.

"I want something with encouraging Bible verses in it," Jan heard Elaine say, "but I don't think any of these are quite the right fit." Elaine crossed her arms, studying the shelf. "I need something a little cheerier."

"I think I've got just the thing," Bristol said, holding up a finger. "But it's going to be over in the youth section. Follow me." Bristol waved for Elaine to come on.

"Of course," Elaine said, tapping her forehead with her palm. "Why didn't I think to look over there?"

Bristol and Jan giggled.

"Avery's pretty mature for her age. I can see why you might have started in the grown-up inspirational section. Don't be so hard on yourself," Jan said.

"You're a tea girl, not a bookshop owner," Bristol said. "That's what I'm here for. If everyone was an expert on my stock, I'd find myself out of a job pretty quickly. Here we are," Bristol said when they got to the kids' section.

Jan loved that section—it was even more colorful than the adult book area and there were chairs and pillows everywhere in bright hues for kids to sit on and enjoy the wide selection of fiction and nonfiction that Bristol stocked, for little ones through teens.

Bristol pulled out a little volume with a soft blue cover and a title printed in bubbly, friendly lettering. Even before she handed it to Elaine and it was opened, Jan could tell Avery would like it.

Elaine flipped through the pages, reading a passage here and there until finally she closed it, looking satisfied. "This is it, Bristol," she said. "It's just the right thing for Avery."

Happy with their selections, Jan and Elaine followed Bristol to the counter. She grabbed the latest copy of Jan's magazine from beneath the desk, and then added up each of their purchases and put them all into a cute little brown paper shopping bag and tied the handles together with a string of twine.

"Here you go, gals," Bristol said, handing over their goodies. "Come back and see me soon."

"We will, I'm sure," Jan said.

They took their purchases, both pleased with their finds, and headed back outside. They'd made it to Elaine's car and almost climbed inside when Jan caught movement out of the corner of her eye. She looked across the street, squinting in an attempt to see better.

"Hey," she said, waving at Elaine. "Do you see that guy over there?"

"Where?" Elaine asked.

"Across the street, over between Gift Me and the library," Jan clarified, pointing as best she could without being too obvious.

"Yes, I see it," Elaine said. "It's far away, but that guy sort of looks familiar, doesn't he?"

"That's what I thought," Jan said. She heard the click of the doors unlocking and Elaine leaned in to open her glove compartment.

"Here, try these," Elaine said, handing a pair of binoculars to Jan, who couldn't help but laugh.

"What on earth do you carry these around for?" Jan asked through her giggles.

"You just never know," Elaine explained, giving a sly grin. "I figure if we're going to be legitimate mystery solvers around here, we've got to equip ourselves with at least some of the gear."

Jan rolled her eyes, but put the binoculars to quick use. It took a moment for the scene to become clear through the thick lenses, but eventually she was able to adjust them.

"Hey!" Jan said. "It's that guy from the show—from *Treasure Travels*."

"Which guy?" Elaine asked. "Stuart or Gary?"

"Neither," Jan answered. "It's that other guy, the guest. Adam what's-his-name? I can't remember."

"Adam Watkins?" Elaine asked. "The professor?"

"That's the one," Jan said. "At least I'm pretty sure." He had the same hunched-over posture, the same thin frame that wasn't wiry from vigorous activity, but rather from a lack thereof, as if he spent all of his time indoors. It made sense for a professor, Jan supposed. All that studying.

"What's he doing over here, I wonder?" Elaine mused out loud. "Let me see those."

Jan handed over the binoculars so Elaine could take a look. "That's him all right."

"Maybe he's been working in the library," Jan suggested. "Rose did mention he'd been over there when she stopped by for a recipe book."

"Maybe so," Elaine said. "But if so, what's that giant thing in the back of his truck?" She handed the binoculars back to Jan.

"I didn't even look closely at his truck before. How do you know it's his?" she asked, working to refocus.

"The fact that he was getting out of it a second ago is a pretty good indication," Elaine teased.

Finally, Jan saw what Elaine was talking about. Sure enough, there was Watkins, whose face she remembered from the television show. He was fiddling with something behind the passenger seat of the cab, and then he stopped doing that and climbed inside.

"Isn't it kind of strange for a professor of history to be driving a big farm truck like that?" Jan asked, checking out the front of the cab and noting the double wheels at the back.

"What's even stranger," Elaine said, "is what's in the back."

Jan scanned the binoculars over and inhaled a rapid breath. "Oh, I see it!"

"What does that look like to you?" Elaine asked as Jan caught a glimpse of a large object standing in the bed of the pickup, a thick blanket obscuring whatever was under it from view.

Jan pulled the lenses away from her face, staring at her cousin in shock.

"Looks an awful lot like it could be a statue!" Jan whispered.

"The question is," Elaine said. "What are we going to do now?"

Jan shook her head, handing back the binoculars. "I have no idea. Should we call the police?"

The two women climbed into the car and waited.

"Of course we should, as soon as know anything for sure. After all, whatever's in the back of that truck could be absolutely anything, and we have no concrete evidence that Mr. Watkins has done anything suspicious," Elaine reasoned.

"Let's see," Jan said. "What do we know about him so far?"

"Well, they showed his photo on the preview of the next *Treasure Travels* the other day, and the Hendersons said they'd consulted with him on the statue because of the book he'd written. By the way, have you gotten a chance to read any of it yet?" Elaine asked. "I meant to, but we've been so busy."

"I didn't read much. It's not exactly inviting," Jan said. "But I did skim through and it seems to be a lot of kooky theories about how the Camden statue went missing originally, how he believes it belongs in Augusta because Camden was from there, and so on."

"And Keira from the Corinth said he'd been carrying around a notebook that he was overly protective of. Maybe he's got more wild ideas in there," Elaine added, sounding doubtful. "But he's just a history professor. Why would he want to steal a historical artifact instead of letting it go to someone who would put it somewhere to ensure that the public could enjoy it?"

"I don't know," Jan answered. "Beats me."

"What motive does he have to take the statue anyway? Could he really just be here to do an educational interview with the Hendersons?" Elaine pondered.

"Or maybe he got wind of the fact that the statue was going to the library here and he wanted to come and see it for himself. It does seem like if you studied something all your working life, you might actually want to take a peek at it in person," Jan said. She wasn't convinced that the professor had any real reason to take the statue. Still, she thought, what was that huge thing doing in the back of his truck if he was just in town for an interview?

"Wait!" Elaine said. "He's leaving!"

"Well, we'd better call Trooper Benson fast, then," Jan said, pulling her phone out of her bag.

"Not yet," Elaine cautioned. "I think we should wait until we have something more definite to tell him."

"Are you saying what I think you're saying?" Jan asked, hearing the excitement in her own voice, then trying to temper it. "If he really is the thief, we could be at risk of getting hurt."

"I don't think a skinny professor is going to do anything to us," Elaine said. "The worst he could do is whack us over the heads with that giant book of his."

"All right, I'm all in. I just feel I should go on record as saying that this whole idea is a little crazy," Jan said. "If Nathan finds out, or if Dan gets upset with us for getting too heavily involved with too little information, then it's on you."

"Duly noted," Elaine said, but her eyes were on the road, laser focused straight ahead.

"But I'm only agreeing to this on one condition," Jan added.

"What's that?" Elaine asked, briefly glancing over.

"That we don't approach the suspect," Jan said.

"It's a deal."

Elaine winked at her cousin as they followed Watkins's truck from a safe distance, if there was such a thing.

CHAPTER FIFTEEN

"Do you think we should just keep driving?" Jan asked, catching the look of steely determination on her cousin's face. "We could end up in Timbuktu."

"He's got to stop soon," Elaine argued. "He can't be going far. I don't even think they've interviewed him for *Treasure Travels* yet. It seemed like Serina was going to go first."

"What if the Hendersons have already recorded his segment?" Jan asked. "This could end up being a wild goose chase."

"Then at least we'll rule him out as a suspect," Elaine said, waving a hand to brush off Jan's comment.

Jan glanced over at her cousin. "It's just that I'm a little worried about how deep into this you've gotten. I know we've worked on plenty of mysteries together, but this one's... different for you, and I know it's been hard."

Elaine's mouth formed a thin line. "I'm not going to quit until we know who stole that statue. Besides, this is by far *not* the craziest thing we've gotten ourselves into."

"I can't argue with that," Jan agreed.

Just ahead of them, Watkins's truck slowed and turned into a driveway. They followed him into a lot lined with buildings that looked like garages—a storage facility!

"I think we've hit the jackpot," Elaine said, pulling her car into a spot far away from where Watkins parked.

"Or we've met our ends," Jan said as they sat still in the car, careful not to draw attention. "And this is where he'll hide our bodies."

"Don't be silly," Elaine said. "There are two of us and one of him. He won't harm us. Besides, he doesn't even know who we are, remember? We've never met. As far as he's concerned we're just two women of a certain age, stopping in to drop off a bag of yarn or some quilts or something. He'll never be able to figure out what we're really doing here."

Elaine was right on that point, and Jan was able to take some comfort in that fact. On their end, they were suspicious of Watkins, but he didn't know them from Adam—or Eve, as the case may be—so there was nothing in their visit to the storage facility to draw suspicion, though keeping that thought in mind proved more difficult than Jan expected when her cousin opened the driver's side door and got out of the car.

"He's on the move," Elaine said. "We've got to go after him."

Jan followed Elaine. At first, they just strolled along, keeping an unobtrusive eye on Watkins, but then he rounded a corner and Elaine crouched against the wall of the building and continued after him before he could get out of their sight.

"Be careful," Jan whispered to Elaine, who just waved a hand behind her back.

After winding up and down several corridors to keep up with Watkins, the cousins saw him stop in front of a doorway near the back. He glanced around before opening the door, but from where they stood, Jan and Elaine couldn't see anything.

"See," Jan said, "I told you this wasn't going to help."

"I think he's just looking in there to check on his stuff. He'll have to go back to his truck and bring over whatever's in the bed," Elaine said hopefully.

"I guess that's a good thing," Jan added, "because we forgot to bring the binoculars anyway."

Elaine looked over at her cousin and gave a little laugh. "You're right. We left them back in my car. When he goes back that way, we'll follow him and pick them up."

"Okay," Jan said.

Sure enough, Watkins, looking satisfied with the contents of what they assumed was his unit, turned and headed back their way. They had gotten themselves stuck in a little groove in the wall and Jan hoped they were hidden by the shadows. They held their breath as he passed by, and Elaine gave her a relieved look when he was gone.

"That was close," Jan said as they left the hiding spot and began to follow Watkins.

Back at the parking lot, they retrieved the binoculars stealthily and then did the whole thing over again, as if one time wasn't bad enough. This time, when Watkins opened the storage unit door, Elaine was ready to peer inside.

"What do you see in there?" Jan asked as her cousin squinted into the eyepieces.

"Just a bunch of old junk, from what I can tell. It looks like the inside of any ordinary family's attic," Elaine said, but Jan wanted more detail.

"Can you make out anything specific?" Jan asked.

"I think—yes, it is," Elaine said.

"What?" Jan asked, more insistently this time.

"It's a mannequin, kind of like some of the ones we saw in Harrison's store. Remember, he said someone had bought one recently?"

"How do you know if it's the same one?"

Elaine turned a few knobs on the binoculars and took a couple of steps closer, still keeping their spot behind a corner to stay out of Watkins's line of vision. "It's wearing a wedding gown. Remember? Harrison said the person who bought a mannequin from him that day needed it for an old wedding dress."

"So, Watkins was there in the shop the day the thief took the lumberjack mannequin to use in place of the statue to fool the board, but the mannequin in his storage unit is the one that Harrison sold legitimately, and it's wearing a wedding dress," Jan said, confusion setting in. "Of course, it could just be a coincidence that the theft and the purchase happened on the same day."

She took the binoculars and focused them back on what Watkins was doing. He still hadn't taken the blanket off whatever was in the back of his truck, and he hadn't made a move to get it into his storage unit yet, so there was still hope.

"I think he's going to take off the cover!" she whispered as loudly as she could without risking being heard.

They looked at each other with shared expressions of anticipation.

"This could be it," Elaine said as Jan handed back the binoculars. They weren't so far away that she couldn't vaguely see what was going on.

They grew eerily silent and the tension was almost palpable as Watkins grabbed two corners and slowly pulled the cover off the pile.

"Is it the statue?" Jan asked, but Elaine didn't answer. She was staring straight ahead, the binoculars resting in a hand at her side, looking for all the world as if her last hope had been shattered.

"No," Elaine said, her voice flat. "It's just a stack of crates full of books, tied up with rope. It's not the statue."

OKAY, LORD, JAN prayed silently. *We're at a loss for a next move here, so anything would help. Amen.*

Jan had to admit she'd been hoping to find something in Watkins's storage unit to incriminate him. She truly had no idea what to do next to try and solve the case so Nathan could be cleared and Elaine could rest easy, and they were all running out of time. The library fund-raiser was just over a week away.

"Do you think we should call Dan?" Elaine asked as she drove.

"What are we going to tell him?" Jan asked.

"I don't know. I think it's a little suspicious that Watkins just happened to be in Harrison's store the same day that the mannequin the thief put in place of the Camden statue was stolen, don't you?"

"Yes, I do think it's strange, but it's not enough to make Watkins guilty. Harrison did say some guy bought a mannequin that day, fair and square, and he did say that guy planned to use it to hold a wedding dress," Jan pointed out.

"I know, I know," Elaine said, "but I still don't think it would hurt to talk to Dan anyway."

Jan nodded and pulled out her phone. She waited on hold until Trooper Benson came on the line to talk with her.

"Hi, there, Jan," he greeted. "I'll just tell you up front that we don't have any new information on that Camden statue. We're still working hard, but it's a tough one."

"I'm sorry to hear that, Dan," she said. "But there's something Elaine and I wanted to share with you."

"Oh yeah?" Dan asked, his tone friendly and curious.

"Yes. We know it probably won't amount to anything, but we've discovered something odd and we just thought we'd pass it on so you could make a decision on whether to look into it or not," Jan began.

"All right, I'm all ears," Dan prompted.

She explained Watkins's relevancy to the Camden statue and that they had seen the man with what appeared to be a large object in the back of his truck that looked like it might be the statue itself, and that they had decided to follow the professor. Dan wasn't too happy about that, but they hadn't done anything against the law. He let it go, but not before giving Jan a stern warning that she and her cousin ought not to be following strange men around on suspicion.

"I know." She gave Elaine a stern look across the car. "But we really thought that might have been the statue in the back of his truck."

"But it wasn't, was it?" Dan clarified.

"No," Jan said sadly. "However, we do know that Adam Watkins was in Harrison Ellerby's shop the same day someone stole a mannequin—matching the one we found in the stolen statue's place—from the store."

"I see," Dan said. "But the problem is that Watkins had a different reason for being in the store that day. We caught the same lead you did and questioned Steve, Ellerby, and Watkins." Dan paused, letting things sink in. "When we talked to the professor, he said he bought a mannequin from Ellerby to hold his mother's old wedding gown because she's moving from her house in Augusta into a new place."

Dan continued. "Watkins voluntarily allowed us to search his storage unit, and we didn't find anything untoward, so as far as we're concerned, he's clear, and we've all but ruled him out as a suspect."

CHAPTER SIXTEEN

After following Watkins to his storage unit and hearing from Trooper Benson, Elaine had begun to wonder if it was time for her and Jan to give up on sleuthing. But she was glad they had followed Watkins. At least she'd been able to see for herself that he wasn't in possession of the statue.

She'd spoken with Nathan a little bit after she and Jan returned home, mostly just to catch him up on the news that they still hadn't found anything concrete, but that they were still hopeful. Each time she thought she was on to something, it turned out to be a dead end, but a still, small voice told her not to lose heart, and to be patient, and she knew at the very deepest part of her heart that Nathan wasn't involved, and that she could trust him.

What she needed was a longer-than-usual quiet time with God—a mini retreat of sorts—to spend time some extra time praying and listening. She'd been giving Avery all this advice about how to lean in to the Lord, how to lay her troubles at His feet, and there was a reason she'd passed that truth along: the best thing to do was to give it all over to Him.

She decided that the next afternoon, after she and Jan had finished clearing up from the day's work, was the perfect chance to take a break. Jan was having a cup of tea at the kitchen table while working on a puzzle in her new issue of *Cryptograms*, so Elaine took the opportunity for solitude and headed upstairs to their parlor, stopping at her room to grab her Bible from the bedside table.

She went into the parlor and turned on a lamp before curling up on the sofa and covering her lap with a quilt Jan had sewn. Flipping through the book, she noticed all the passages she'd highlighted over the years—a road map of her own and her family's joy and pain. It was beautiful, really, to see all of the promises that had brought her comfort and soothed her soul during the most difficult times of her life, and the happiest.

Finally, not really knowing how she'd landed there, she settled on one passage in particular—John 14:26–27: "But the Comforter, which is the Holy Ghost, whom the Father will send in my name, he shall teach you all things, and bring all things to your remembrance, whatsoever I have said unto you. Peace I leave with you, my peace I give unto you: not as the world giveth, give I unto you. Let not your heart be troubled, neither let it be afraid."

It was so lovely, and so needed, that it almost brought tears to her eyes. Elaine prayed the passage over herself, and then over Nathan, wanting her loved one to feel the comfort she felt in God's Word, even if he wasn't there beside her to see it.

After a few moments to herself, Elaine heard Jan come in, and she was glad to see her standing in the doorway.

"Hey," Jan said softly, her eyes landing on the open Bible in Elaine's lap. "Am I interrupting?"

"No," Elaine said, "I'm finished here. Just needed a little quiet time to remind myself of who I am and Who's in charge here."

Jan came in and sat next to her cousin on the couch. "I know what you mean. Listen," she said, sounding energized. "I have an idea."

"What?" Elaine asked. "Is it your turn to take us on a wild car chase?"

Jan laughed. "No, but I hope it's not a wild goose chase either."

"Whatever it is, I'm sure it won't be as nutty as what I put us through yesterday."

"No, probably not," Jan agreed with a grin.

"So, what have you got for us?" Elaine asked, feeling replenished after her time alone with the Word and ready to move on.

"I was thinking I'd head back to Waterville and visit the docks," Jan explained.

"The docks?" Elaine asked, unsure where Jan's plan was headed.

"Yes," Jan said, folding her hands in her lap. "I was sitting there working puzzles when out of the blue I remembered Serina Frost saying that she'd found the plaque *down at the docks*."

"That's right," Elaine said, "she did."

Jan nodded. "I figure if she was only staying at the Corinth for a few days and wasn't there to tour for fun, she probably didn't venture too far from the hotel, and there are only so many docks around there."

"I'm tracking with you, but what do you think we'll gain by going down there ourselves?"

"Well," Jan said, "all this time we've been operating under the assumption that the statue is here"—she pushed a finger into the couch for emphasis—"on dry land."

Elaine's eyes narrowed. "I'm not sure I understand."

"What if it's not here?" Jan asked. "What if the plaque fell off the statue when someone was handling it near the water and it's floating down the Kennebec somewhere, or it's already made its way to the Gulf, even?"

"That would just be terrible," Elaine said. "If that's true, we don't even stand a chance of getting it back—ever—much less in time for the library fund-raiser."

Jan nodded solemnly. "I know," she said. "But why else would she have found the plaque down there? And don't you think it would be best if we at least knew for sure that what we're spending so much time and energy searching for is, in fact, able to be found?"

"I guess you have a point," Elaine agreed. "But how do you intend to find that out from the docks?"

"Come with me," Jan said, "and I'll tell you on the way there."

"So, has Clifton got back to you yet about where you'll go to lunch?" Elaine asked Jan as her cousin drove them to Waterville.

"The Pine Tree Grill," Jan answered. "I'd almost forgotten about it, what with all this going on. But the more I think about it, the more relaxed I feel about the idea of spending time with him."

"Yeah?" Elaine asked. "That's good to hear."

Jan smiled, her eyes sticking to the road. "You know, Rose is such a wonderful young woman and he took part in raising her, so how bad can he be?"

"That is a dangerous question, my friend," Elaine said, causing Jan to chuckle. "But in all seriousness, I think you're probably right. He is a really decent man."

"Yes, he is," Jan agreed, glancing over at her cousin with a serious expression. "I guess if it turns out we do like each other in the same way, then I can try to figure out how to tackle the problem of having two good men interested in me."

"That is a tough one," Elaine said, not joking. "But it's just lunch, and you don't have to decide anything until after you go. It may even take longer than that."

Jan sighed.

"But whatever is supposed to happen, just listen to God. He'll be right there beside you to help you figure it out."

"I know, and I agree one hundred percent that He will be with me in spirit, but I wish, well, I wish I could *see* Him there with me too. Wouldn't things be so much easier if God came with Clifton and me out to lunch and I could just lean over and ask Him what He thought and what I should do?"

Elaine had to chuckle at the image her cousin had painted. "Yes, it certainly would be," she said. "I think that applies in a lot of situations."

Just a few minutes later, Jan turned off the highway onto a road that led down to the Kennebec River and eased the car into a lot with a few other cars. The sounds of ship horns and heavy machinery greeted them as the cousins got out of the car. Jan clicked the lock behind her as they walked toward a small building at the edge of the marina. When they got close, a man opened a little window and greeted them.

"Hi," he said. "I'm Tom. What can I do for you today?"

Elaine nodded at Jan, silently telling her to go ahead.

"We're from Lancaster, just up the highway, and something's happened recently that's rocked our little community quite a bit."

"I'm sorry to hear that," Tom said.

"You may have heard about the disappearance of a statue of Phillip Camden?" Jan asked.

Tom looked off into the distance for a second, thinking. "You know, I did read something about that in the paper and it's just awful. I was a big reader of his as a boy—had all his books and loved them. I was sorry to hear about that statue getting stolen. It's a shame what people will do for money these days."

Jan nodded. "I know you are probably limited in what you can share with strangers, but along those lines, I wonder if you might be able to tell us if you're aware of any recent shipments of particularly large, unusual objects."

Tom put a hand to his chin. "You know, we get so much traffic in here and we switch shifts, so I can't recall, but if you'll give me a moment, I'll go check the logs for you. I won't be able to tell you any specifics, but I can let you know if we've had anything out of the norm pass through here."

"Anything will help," Jan said.

Tom nodded and headed back to his watch building, leaving Jan and Elaine to wait restlessly for his return. When he got back, Elaine studied his features for any sign of what news he was bringing, but when he got closer, he shook his head.

"Nothing, huh?" Elaine asked.

"Nothing unusual. Just the normal cargo we see through here all the time—oil, frozen goods, supplies. One of us has to check each ship and the notes don't indicate anything out of the ordinary," Tom said. Elaine was touched at his tone—he seemed disappointed at having to let them down.

"Well, we certainly appreciate your checking," Jan said.

"Anytime," Tom said, nodding.

"One more thing?" Elaine asked. "You wouldn't happen to know about any...off the books...shipments that go on around here?"

Tom's expression was adamantly distraught. "Oh no, ma'am," he said, shaking his head vigorously. "I wouldn't know anything about that and neither would any of the other men. We run a clean dock here and wouldn't take kindly to any sort of criminal activity. I assure you, anything like that would be reported to the police immediately."

"I'm sure it would," Jan said, soothing his ruffled feathers. "And we meant no offense. We're just looking for answers."

Tom's shoulders lowered and he seemed appeased. "Of course," he said, "I understand. I'm sorry I wasn't able to help."

"Oh, no, Tom, you have helped," Jan said, smiling warmly.

They both thanked him and headed back to the car.

"Well, that was a bust," Elaine said, not surprised. Every potential clue seemed to lead to the same place lately—nowhere.

"Not necessarily," Jan said, unlocking the car doors. "It reminded me of something else. Something that may very well turn out to be our next clue."

CHAPTER SEVENTEEN

J an drove home as quickly as traffic would allow, eager to get back so she could check on her theory.

When they pulled into the drive, she parked the car quickly and she and Elaine rushed inside, still in their coats as they headed for the hallway. Jan reached into the jar she'd been keeping on a table near the door and pulled out all the business cards she could in one handful, then leaned down to spread them out on the floor.

"Is it in there?" Elaine asked, crouching next to her.

"I haven't seen it yet—if I remember correctly, I think it might be light blue," she answered.

Elaine put her hands into the fray and shuffled the cards around as well. "Aha!" she said, holding up a pale-blue business card with the words *Mainely Movers* printed on the front, along with a phone number and e-mail address. It was wrinkled and soft-looking from being crunched up in a man's wallet.

"That's it," Jan said, stopping her own search to put all the cards back into the jar except the one she needed.

"So, what do we do now?" Elaine asked, reaching out for Jan to take the card from her.

"Well, it's a long shot," Jan said, examining the paper in her hand, "but I remember these young college-age guys coming in just before you got back from the library on the day the statue was taken. And I recall them saying they had a job here in town that made them uneasy, and they were in a hurry to get to Augusta. The job was something big and heavy they had agreed to carry at the last minute for an extra-large fee. It sounded weird to me at the time, but I guess I didn't connect the dots, because I didn't think anything of it, until now. The timing would be correct if it was them."

"So, it's possible they were talking about the Camden statue," Elaine said.

"Yes, I think it is," Jan said, trying not to let herself get too excited in case this turned out to be yet another dead end. She didn't want Elaine getting her hopes too high either.

"It would make sense, considering Serina found the plaque down by the docks—maybe it fell off in the move," Elaine reasoned.

"Right, that's what I'm thinking too." Jan frowned. "The only problem is, if the statue was down by the docks for some reason, and if the plaque fell off, then why was it there to begin with?"

Elaine's brows knit. "Good question. Especially considering that Tom at the docks said he didn't see anything matching the description getting shipped off and he said the logbook didn't show anything either." She paused, then her eyes widened. "Maybe they still had the statue in the truck from the night before, and when they stopped to pick up something else at the dock on their way out of town, the plaque fell off of the truck before they drove back to Augusta."

"That's definitely a possibility, and it would explain how Serina came across the plaque if it was lying there on the ground. I feel like we're close to a breakthrough, but we're missing a piece and I can't for the life of me figure out what it is."

"I feel the same way," Elaine said, nodding.

Jan stood and placed the jar on the counter, then offered a hand to help Elaine up from the floor.

"The only way to find out if the pieces fit or not is to give these guys a call and go from there," Jan said, pulling her cell phone out of her purse and then punching in the number on the card. "Here goes."

THE NEXT DAY, Jan was sitting across from Clifton at the Pine Tree Grill, grateful for the distraction from constantly checking her phone. She'd left at least three messages at the number for Mainely Movers, and she was dying to hear back, so when Clifton called that morning to ask if she'd be free for a late lunch after the tearoom crowd calmed, she agreed.

He'd looked nice when he arrived to pick her up, and she'd been looking forward to spending some time with him, but once they'd gotten past pleasant greetings, the conversation had quickly waned, and Jan found herself searching for topics to talk about beyond Rose, orthodontia, and the tearoom. He was a good man—gentle and kind—but when he'd held out a hand to help her out of his car at the restaurant, she noticed that she hadn't felt anything. Perhaps that was normal, but in her heart, she'd been waiting to see if there was that little something…a spark…like she felt when Bob held her hand or put a palm to her elbow to help her over a step. She couldn't decide if she was surprised or pleased to discover that it was missing with Clifton.

Clifton smiled at her from across the table, and looked as if he was about to speak, but then Bianca Stadler arrived with their burgers and Jan recognized her own feeling of relief in his expression. He commented on how great their food smelled, she agreed, and then they ate quietly for a few moments, each glancing around at decorations on the log walls. Jan couldn't help but think that with Bob, the silence would have been companionable, whereas with Clifton, as wonderful a person he was, it wasn't quite as comfortable.

"So," Jan said, leaving her meal for a moment to take a sip of her water. "Rose seems to be enjoying herself in culinary school."

Clifton nodded, grinning as he put down his hamburger. "Oh, she is. I don't think I've ever seen her so happy."

"Of course, that has a lot to do with the new man in her life, I think," Jan said.

"You're right about that," Clifton answered with a chuckle. "As a father, I know I'm supposed to be wary of anyone my girl dates, but it's hard to feel that way about Brent. He's a great guy, and Rose just loves his kiddo."

"Yes," Jan said. "I'm so happy to see her thriving after…well, you know." Jan mentally kicked herself. She hadn't meant to bring up the sensitive subject of Rose's mother's passing, but Clifton just nodded agreeably.

"I am too. It was definitely hard on us. Rose's mother and I had just patched things up after several difficult months, and I was looking forward to a future with her," he said sadly, a faraway look in his eyes that Jan recognized.

Even though it was in a different way, she was missing someone too.

"You miss her, don't you?" Jan asked, knowing the answer was obvious but wanting to show Clifton that she understood his sadness.

He nodded, his eyes soft. "Yes, I do. You know, Jan, I thought I was ready for something new with someone new, but it's harder than I thought."

Jan wasn't sure that they were on the same page about *why* exactly dating someone new was difficult, but she felt the exact same way.

She shook her head and reached across the table to gently pat the top of his hand where it rested. "It's okay. You don't have to say more. I'm there too. Even though I understood Bob's reason for taking a job offer out of town, and even though I still support him, it's been harder than I thought it would be, having him so far away."

Clifton studied her as she took a sip of her water. "You know what they say—absence makes the heart grow fonder."

Jan grinned and set down her glass. "I guess that's true in this case," she said, sad for Clifton that he wouldn't be able to rejoin his late wife.

"What a pair we are," Clifton suggested.

"All we can do is talk about the ones we're missing," Jan said. "I suppose that should tell us something."

"That our hearts are both somewhere else today, aren't they?" he mused pleasantly.

That wasn't quite what she'd meant, as she thought her heart might be somewhere else—with Bob—*permanently*, but Jan smiled anyway.

A few moments passed and finally Bianca brought the check, then wished them both a happy rest of the day.

As he walked her out to his Honda to take her back to the tearoom, Clifton seemed relaxed, and Jan wasn't sure what to think about how things had gone. She couldn't decide exactly how she felt, or if she would want to go out with Clifton again.

Clifton nodded and held the car door open for her. "I had a great time with you," he said. "Perhaps we should go to dinner soon?"

Jan smiled as a ray of sun peeked through the clouds over the restaurant. "That would be nice," she said, returning Clifton's smile. She just had to figure out first if it should be just as friends.

JAN WAS IN the kitchen the next morning, preparing dough for the day's first batch of mini maple croissants, when she heard a light knock at the kitchen door. She brushed her floury hands on her apron and hurried to answer it. Geraldine was just raising her hand to knock again.

"Oh, hi, Geraldine," Jan greeted, swinging the door wide and gesturing her inside. "Come on in! How are you this morning?"

"Hi there, Jan," she said, reaching out to take Jan's outstretched hand. "It's nice to see you."

"Archie and Elaine are dusting in the parlors. Would you like me to show you in?" Jan asked.

"If you would be so kind," Geraldine said. "He said to stop by whenever I like—I hope I'm not imposing."

Jan waved that statement away. "Absolutely not. We love having you here," she said, making Geraldine smile.

Jan pulled off her apron and hung it on one of the cabinet knobs underneath the counter near her mixing bowl, then showed Geraldine into the parlor where Archie was reaching to dust a tall curio cabinet and Elaine was on the other side, straightening a tablecloth.

"Archie," Jan called, "Geraldine's here to see you."

Archie stopped what he was doing, put down his dusting rag and spray, and turned, smiling when he saw Geraldine. They really did have the same eyes, Jan thought, and there was something in the way they carried themselves when they walked that was strikingly similar.

"It's so nice to see you," Archie said. "Do come and sit down."

"Hello, Geraldine," Elaine said, giving a little wave. "I'll run into the kitchen and get you both some tea so you can visit."

"That would be so kind of you," Geraldine said, and Archie echoed her thanks, shooting Elaine a look of gratitude.

Jan followed her cousin into the kitchen, where she slipped a sheet of croissants into the preheated oven. "I'll have to wait until these come out to give them something to munch on. I don't want to give Geraldine yesterday's pastries."

"What kind of tea do you think she'd like this morning?" Elaine asked. "I didn't think to ask when we were out there."

"Probably something strong," Jan guessed. "They're treading through some difficult areas, so she might need it."

Elaine nodded and made a pot of plain orange pekoe. Jan finished her dough and followed closely behind.

Archie and Geraldine were hunched together when the two women joined them, looking like two peas in a pod. Jan and Elaine sat for a quick cup of tea with them.

"Geraldine and I are figuring out that we have so much in common," Archie said, a giddiness in his voice.

"Like what?" Jan asked.

The two shared a glance.

"Well," Geraldine said, "aside from the pecan allergy, we've discovered we both absolutely despise brussels sprouts." She giggled. "I've never been able to stand the little beasts. My mother always told me I'd outgrow it and develop a taste for them as an adult, but it simply never happened."

Archie laughed. "I'm the same way. I cannot stomach them for the life of me, and it's only partly because they look like cabbages that shrunk somehow."

Geraldine giggled and added milk and sugar to her tea, then took a sip, closing her eyes as she drank in the bracing liquid. "Ah, strong and robust, just the way I like it," she said.

"What else have you discovered?" Elaine asked, as curious as a child.

Jan had to admit—their camaraderie was contagious. Initially they had all been a little leery of the woman who'd shown up out of the blue to ask after a painting they had bought fair and square, but now, she could easily see that very same woman becoming a part of all of their lives.

Archie's eyes lit up when he was around her, and the two were developing a very dear friendship. Jan knew there had to be something to it, and she hoped they'd figure it out soon.

Geraldine turned solemn and shared a glance with Archie. "I think," she said tentatively, "that we've decided to go ahead and both get DNA testing to find out if we might be related."

Archie nodded. "I've talked it over with Gloria," he said, referring to his wife. "It's a serious step, but I think we're both ready to find out the truth."

"I haven't had much success in learning about my adoption," Geraldine said, "but one of the only things I've been able to piece together from my adoptive parents is that my birth father served in the war, and something happened to my mother while he was away—she died, you see, and that's how I came to live with my parents, who were unable to have children. Then, of course, I grew up, got married, and settled over here in Maine."

Jan and Elaine shared a look. "We're both hoping you find out more and more, and we'll be praying for answers for you," Elaine said.

"Thank you," Geraldine said. "You've been so kind."

"Well," Jan said, "it's been our pleasure to have you around, and we hope we'll be seeing a lot more of you."

Jan and Elaine stood up and gathered some of the used tea things, then returned to the kitchen to let Archie and Geraldine have some time to talk privately.

Later that afternoon, after a busy day, Paula brought Avery by the tearoom after school while Kelly attended her karate lesson. Things had calmed down, so after saying hello and getting a glass of chocolate milk for Avery and a cup of tea for Paula, Jan told Elaine she would take care of the few remaining customers while Elaine went to give her granddaughter the book. When everyone had been served and Archie had things under control, Jan finished what she was doing in the kitchen and decided the rest could wait until later. She went upstairs to the parlor to join her family.

Avery was flipping through her new book when Jan came to sit at their table.

"Look what I got, Grandma," she said proudly, holding up the little blue volume of verses for Jan to admire.

"Yes, that's a beautiful gift," Jan agreed. "Did you say thank you?"

Paula nodded over Avery's head and Avery nodded too.

The four women chatted for a few minutes and then Elaine got a look in her eye that Jan recognized as resolve. Whatever it was she had in mind, Jan knew Elaine would see that it came to fruition.

"I have an idea," Elaine said. "Why don't you and your mom go out to the car and get your cello."

Surprise and confusion blended in Avery's features. "What for?" she asked. "I already had practice today."

"I know you did," Elaine said, "but, if it's okay with you, I think you should try playing your solo for the customers."

At first, Jan thought her granddaughter would vehemently disagree with the suggestion, but as she thought about it, her expression began to brighten.

"You know," Avery said, crossing her arms and studying the ceiling, "it's not a bad idea."

"That's our girl!" Elaine exclaimed.

Paula looked pleased and headed off to get the instrument, telling Avery to stay there.

"I think it might actually help," Avery said. "I have to play in front of a crowd again soon, anyway, and this one isn't so big or scary."

"Yeah," Elaine encouraged, "it's a great place to get back on the horse again."

Avery scrunched up her nose. "Horse? What horse?"

Jan and Elaine shared a laugh. "It's an old expression," Jan explained. "It just means trying something once more after a hard time with it."

"Oh," Avery said, "I get it."

Paula returned with the instrument a moment later, and Avery set up near the front of the east parlor. The customers shuffled in their seats, turning to see what was going on, and Jan was pleased to see interested curiosity in their faces.

Once Avery had her cello ready to go, she plucked the strings a few times, which was enough introduction in itself to draw attention. All eyes were on Jan's granddaughter, and Jan's heart swelled with pride as Avery hit note after note in perfect tune. And when she made it through the whole of her solo without a single moment of struggle, Jan was the first of many to stand and clap her heart out.

"You did great!" Elaine called out as the clapping finally began to subside.

"We knew you could do it," Jan said. "All you had to do was try again."

Avery beamed as her family congratulated her on a job well done, and after another cup of chocolate milk and a second well-deserved cookie, she and Paula said their goodbyes and headed back to Augusta.

Elaine had already gone upstairs to get ready for a date with Nathan, and Jan's foot had just landed on the last step upstairs when she heard a faint buzzing from somewhere far off. It took a moment to realize it was her cell phone. She rushed to her bedroom, where she'd left it on the bureau to charge, and picked it up on the last chime. Her heart did a little flip when she saw Bob's name. She pressed her thumb onto the glass to unlock the phone and opened up his text, which asked her if she was available for a quick video chat. She responded yes and then clicked the button.

A moment later, Jan heard the little chime letting her know that she was receiving an incoming call, and then there was Bob, handsome as ever in a business suit and tie.

"Hi there," Jan said, giving a little wave. "How are things?"

Bob waved back and Jan noticed his chocolate-brown eyes seemed to dance. In fact, as they greeted each other and she studied him more closely, he looked as if he was about to burst.

"I really do want to hear about your day," Bob said, his words coming out quick as lightning, "but I just can't wait any longer to tell you the news."

Inside, Jan felt a mix of emotions. Things had been so weird between the two of them lately—almost as if they weren't really connecting anymore—and Jan had been wondering if they could make it with the great distance that separated them. She'd been half expecting Bob to share that he was feeling the same way, and though she wanted them to be open with each other even if something was difficult, she had not been looking forward to such a tough conversation. Watching him speak now, however, she got the feeling he had something entirely different up his sleeve, and she waited with anticipation to find out what it could be.

"Well, what is it?" she asked, holding the phone closer to her face.

Bob's dark eyes went wide as he told her the very thing she'd been waiting so long to hear—the thing she'd been hoping he'd say since the day he'd told her he was moving away.

"I'm coming back, Jan!" he practically shouted into his own phone. "And I can't wait to be back in Lancaster with you again."

Laughing, Jan pulled her phone away from her face at the burst of noise. As much as her heart had sunk back then when he'd told her he was leaving, it soared now.

"The plan is to open my own firm there—the work I've been doing here in Baltimore will translate well to central Maine, and I can't wait to open up there and get started. If all goes well tying up loose ends, I should be home before the end of the month," Bob explained. "Isn't that wonderful?"

"It is—very much so. But what will your partner do if you're leaving? Do you think it will be hard for him to find someone to take your place on such short notice?" Jan asked, then bit her lip. It wouldn't be like Bob to leave without making sure he wasn't causing a burden on his partner.

"That's all settled," Bob answered. "There's a junior lawyer who's been on staff for a while—tremendously talented and hardworking—that they'd love to promote to the position. I'll stay on here for another couple of weeks to make sure the transition is smooth, and then start preparing for the move. Besides, our relationship is more important than staying in Baltimore, and I want to be with you in Lancaster again." He smiled and her heart melted. "Just one thing, though—maybe don't share the news until I've got everything finalized here?"

"I'm so glad to hear it, Bob," she said. "It will be hard keeping it a secret, but I'm very much looking forward to having you back in town."

The mix of emotions she'd been experiencing lately, the uneasy feelings she'd been having about their future, and the drain of the long distance—all faded as Bob went on, relaying more details. And as he joyfully continued to talk about his plans, Jan said a silent thank-you to God for an answered prayer.

CHAPTER EIGHTEEN

Elaine heard Jan speaking to someone on the phone as she finished dressing, grabbed her purse, and headed downstairs. She scribbled a note for her cousin, but Jan already knew about her date with Nathan that night. Remembering at the last minute, Elaine had to rush back upstairs and grab a basket full of items for the fund-raiser that she'd promised Priscilla she would drop off at the library, back before the statue got stolen and threw everything off course. She quickly made her way downstairs again and into the hallway, thinking of her date.

At long last they would have a chance to sit down and talk, to catch up. As she set the basket down and pulled a coat over the dove-gray cowl-neck sweater and navy-blue pants she'd chosen, she said a little prayer, asking that this time together would heal the rift she'd felt between them lately, with the statue theft and Nathan's busy work schedule. She hoped that she and Nathan could speak openly and clear up her worry over why he'd taken so long to text or call her back, and that by the end of their evening together she would feel closer to him.

She felt a little flutter of butterflies in her stomach when she heard the tires of Nathan's shiny black Cadillac in the driveway, and, as he walked up to the porch, she admired how handsome he was in his dark suit and navy tie. His blue eyes danced when he met hers.

"Hey there, stranger," he said, leaning in to kiss her cheek. "Long time no see."

She looked up into his dear face and smiled at him. "It's not for lack of trying on my part," she said, attempting to sound cheerful.

His eyes dimmed. "I know," he said, "and I truly am sorry. I'll explain everything over dinner." He took the basket from her, which she explained, and he agreed to stop at the library on the way back from dinner since he still had the keys Priscilla had given him to get the statue into the building, before it had been taken.

"I'm glad," Elaine said, taking his offered elbow and letting him lead her out to the car. He put her basket on the backseat, then opened the door for her, and when they were seat-belted in, he pulled out onto Main Street and they drove the ten or so miles to Waterville in comfortable quiet.

When they arrived at the Broken Claw, the restaurant that Elaine had chosen—a little seafood place known especially for its delicious fresh lobster rolls—Nathan helped her out of the car and led her inside, always the gentleman. The interior of the restaurant reminded Elaine of a classic English pub, with dark glossy wood, several long tables, and a few softly blazing fireplaces, but it was just slightly more upscale. A hostess led the couple to a small table near one of the fireplaces. As they sat, Elaine noticed the pretty little arrangement of flowers, and a light on the table that looked like an old ship's lantern.

"This place is charming," Elaine said, smiling at Nathan across the table.

"It is," he said, his blue eyes crinkling at the corners. "Excellent choice."

A waiter came just a moment later and took their orders before returning with a basket of fluffy rolls, a coil of steam rising off them, and a bowl of whipped honey butter. Elaine and Nathan each took one and nibbled it before pronouncing them delicious.

After they'd settled in and enjoyed a few bites, Elaine cleared her throat. "How are the boys?" she asked, referring to Nathan's grown sons, Luke and Jacob.

Nathan smiled. "Doing great," he said. "Working hard and staying busy as always, but still finding time to enjoy life."

"Reminds me of someone I know," she said, grinning.

Nathan gave her a soft grin. "And how are things at the tearoom?"

Elaine rolled her eyes and smiled. "Busy as ever. Today in particular. Earlier, Jan and I found out that Archie is going to get DNA testing to find out if he has a long-lost half sibling." She explained all about Geraldine's recent visits and how Archie had come to the conclusion that they could possibly be related. "And Avery stopped by this afternoon. She played her cello for the customers after having a rough rehearsal the other day, and ended up getting a standing ovation."

"That's wonderful," Nathan exclaimed, his roll halfway to his mouth. "I remember you saying she was worried about her upcoming concert and I'm sad to hear that her rehearsal didn't go as well as she wanted, but it sounds like things worked out okay in the end."

"Yes, they did," Elaine said, beaming, proud of Avery. "I think the practice of her solo in front of a supportive crowd did a lot to renew her confidence after the unpleasant experience at rehearsal. I have no doubt that she'll do well on her big night."

Nathan smiled warmly and took a bite of his bread. He swallowed and then sipped his water before speaking.

"Elaine, I know I've been pretty distant lately, and I know my apologies haven't been enough. You deserve an explanation."

Elaine nodded, then took a sip of her own water to quell the sudden dryness in her mouth.

"The reason I've been so busy is because of a doctor's appointment," he said.

Elaine's heart lurched. "Oh," she said, startled at the mention of a medical appointment. Immediately, she began to worry over his health. Nathan had always taken good care of himself; he ate well and exercised regularly. She knew he went to an annual physical exam, but he had never mentioned any particular concerns, so she'd never had reason to ask.

"You see, I had a doctor's appointment the afternoon before the statue was taken," Nathan explained carefully, "and was given some troublesome news."

Elaine nodded, swallowing as her throat tightened with concern.

"My doctor told me he'd found a tumor, and that they would need to run some tests to figure out what it was."

Elaine wove her fingers together under the table, trying not to give in to the moisture that gathered behind her eyes as she listened closely.

"So, I agreed, of course, to the tests, which could not be done until the following morning," he said, looking at her pointedly.

"Ah," she said, realization setting in, "the morning of the library board meeting."

Nathan nodded, his expression serious. "Yes, that's the one."

"Except," she began, nervous to ask again after the way he'd reacted to the question the time before, "what about that night? The night you found out about the tumor?"

"It's simple, really. I had one more appointment that day— with Ellerby, to discuss a few antique pieces I'd purchased recently and was interested in selling. I figured it would be a good distraction from what I'd just heard, so I met with him and then I went home. I was still in the clothes I'd worn to the doctor—workout clothes that are more comfortable to change in and out of than my usual business wear—and I decided to go for a run to clear my head."

Elaine nodded, finally understanding, as tears filled her eyes.

"I ran for over an hour," he said, "just thinking about the life I have and how much I love it"—he looked up at her with moisture in his own eyes—"how much I love you. And then I went home and said a prayer and went to bed. I wasn't in a good place, and I was nervous over the tests I'd be having the next morning."

"Speaking of those," she started, her voice catching with emotion, "how did they turn out?"

Her heart raced as she waited for his answer, bracing herself for whatever came next. If he was okay, she would be so grateful, of course, but if he wasn't…if he wasn't, they would get through it together, whatever *it* was.

His face brightened as he gave her a huge, relieved smile, which went even farther than his next words in making her feel better. "I'm okay. The tumor is benign."

She felt her heart lighten and lift, and said a silent prayer of thanks as she returned his smile.

"They're going to remove it just to be doubly safe, but everything is all right. Surgery is scheduled for a week from now."

"I'm so very glad to hear it's benign, Nathan, and I love you too," she said, reaching across the table to grasp his hand as he visibly relaxed after telling her all that he'd been holding on to alone. "But I don't understand. Why didn't you just tell me all of this before?"

He looked down and shook his head. "You know, it seemed like a good idea at the time…I was trying to avoid telling Dan because I didn't want to risk him saying anything to you before I knew what the test results would be. That's silly, I know. But I knew I was innocent so I wasn't worried about being a suspect, and more than anything, I trusted that you and Jan would find the true culprit, so I wasn't concerned about my fate in terms of the statue for even a moment. I knew I was in the best hands and that you and your cousin would investigate every possible avenue."

He gave her hand a tender little squeeze and searched her eyes. "It was wrong of me not to tell you and let you walk that hard road with me, but I was worried about my health, and about the future of our relationship. Not knowing what was going to happen to me made me think about how much you've come to mean to me, and the unknown of it made me want to distance myself from you. You see, I was so afraid of hurting you."

"I was so worried, though, Nathan," Elaine said softly. "I trust you and I would never believe that you stole the statue."

He let go of her hand and leaned back, looking relieved. "I'm so glad to hear that."

Elaine's brows knit. "But I wish you would have let me be there for you."

He nodded his head in agreement. "I know, and I should have. I'm sorry I wasn't open the way I should have been."

"I'm going to be right by your side when you get out of that surgery."

Nathan smiled, nodding *yes*, and she squeezed his hand and then closed her eyes, glad that everything was okay, and that he was as healthy as ever.

After opening them again, Elaine took a sip of her water as she ruminated on all the new information she'd just received, feeling a complicated combination of emotions that took a moment to articulate. "I'm still a little hurt that you didn't trust me with all of that. It would have given me peace over the last week to know exactly what was going on in your life, but more than that, I'm glad that you're going to be around for a while longer."

Nathan's blue eyes softened. "I'm so sorry," he said again. "Can you forgive me?"

Elaine paused, then gave him a warm smile just as the waitress arrived with their entrees. "Yes, Nathan, I love you and of course I forgive you."

After offering a quick but heartfelt blessing, they tucked into giant, overstuffed lobster rolls that turned out to be almost as delicious as knowing that their relationship was going to be not just all right, but even stronger than before.

ON THE DRIVE home, Elaine remembered the basket in the backseat. "Oh!" she said. "Don't forget to stop at the library. You still have those keys, don't you?"

Nathan turned briefly toward her, then set his eyes back on the road. "Yes, I still have them. The police returned them to me and I need to give them back to her, but I keep forgetting."

"Well, it worked out in my favor," Elaine said. "I promised Priscilla I'd drop off that stuff weeks ago, and I mean to keep my word, even if the fund-raiser doesn't end up happening."

"That reminds me," Nathan said. "There's something else I meant to tell you over dinner."

"What's that?" she asked.

"I've got a racquetball game this weekend with a guy I met who's in town on business. I ran into him at the courts a couple weeks ago and we got to talking, then decided to play a game together. He seemed like a nice guy and we enjoyed it, so we set up another game. But with the statue missing and the tests and all, I've been putting it off. I didn't want him to think I was intentionally avoiding him, so I called him yesterday and we scheduled a game for this weekend."

"That sounds nice," Elaine said, glad to hear that he'd made a new friend. "What's his name?"

"Adam Watkins," Nathan answered. "He's a history professor, here in town for that *Treasure Travels* show and to research his next book on, of all things, Phillip Camden."

Elaine nearly coughed when she heard the name, and considered telling Nathan how familiar she and Jan were with the man, but decided against it, not wanting to worry Nathan. She had a feeling he wouldn't think it had been a great idea for his girlfriend and her cousin to follow a strange man they suspected—with a glaring lack of proof—of a crime he apparently didn't commit.

Thankfully, the darkness in the car ensured that he didn't see the rose color rising up her neck, and he cheerfully kept talking.

"He's a nice guy, and I enjoyed playing racquetball with him and look forward to doing it again, but he seems a little too involved with his work. He talks a lot about his research on the statue. I asked him if he knew about the theft and he said he did, and I told him that I'd been the lucky one to handle it and that the Lancaster Public Library would be its permanent spot. He didn't seem too interested in talking much about it. Watkins has some strong feelings about it—he seems to think the statue should reside in Augusta because Camden taught at the University of Maine campus there, rather than in Lancaster."

Elaine gave soft noises of acknowledgement as Nathan went on. She was frustrated once again. Watkins seemed to be all over the place, but at the same time, there wasn't any indication that he was anything more than just a very opinionated historian with controversial views. Even she had to admit that didn't make him a criminal.

Nathan slowed the car and pulled off the highway and onto Main Street back in Lancaster, ending their drive at the library. It was dark and quiet, but Elaine just planned to slip in and leave the basket for Priscilla on the front desk.

They got out of the car and she grabbed her basket from the backseat. Nathan retrieved the keys Priscilla had given him from his pocket and they headed to the door.

Nathan reached out and put a key into the lock, but when he tried to turn it, the thing wouldn't budge.

"Are you sure it's the right one?" Elaine asked.

"Apparently not," Nathan said, frowning. He searched his ring, sifting through the other keys hanging from it. "Maybe this one. It's newer and shinier than the others. Priscilla thought I might need to get into the storage room with the statue when she was out, but I never actually had to use the keys because she ended up being there to let me in when I had the guys unload it."

Nathan tried different keys, but in the end, none of them seemed to fit in the lock. Elaine grabbed her basket and they headed back to the car.

"Oh well," Nathan said, shrugging. "I guess the key machine got it wrong."

Elaine nodded. She would walk over and drop the basket off tomorrow instead. But as Nathan drove her home, she couldn't shake the feeling that something was wrong.

CHAPTER NINETEEN

The next evening brought Avery's concert. After an exceptionally busy day, Elaine and Jan both had to get cleaned up, get dressed, and drive to Augusta. To make matters worse, they were already running late, which would put them right into the brunt of commuter traffic.

"Jan!" Elaine called up the stairs, at the same time fastening on her wristwatch and scurrying around to locate her purse, which wasn't in its customary spot. She must have moved it sometime during the day and lost track of it with the overload of customers who had flooded in that afternoon. "Are you ready yet, Jan?"

Elaine finally spotted her handbag in her office, but Jan still hadn't come down the stairs.

"All right, last call. We've got to get on the road before we're terribly late," she hollered up the stairs.

Jan appeared at the top of the steps, her cell phone pressed against the palm of one hand. "You go on ahead," she whispered loudly. "I'll meet you there. Save me a seat if you can."

"You're sure?" Elaine asked.

"Yes, yes," Jan said, waving her off as she turned to go back to her room, "I'm sure. Be careful in traffic and I'll see you there."

Having not another second to waste, Elaine put her coat on and hit the road. Traffic was unpleasant but it wasn't as bad as she'd initially worried, and she made it just in time to slide into a seat near the back of the Truman Middle School auditorium before the audience quieted down in anticipation of the show.

As she let go of the tension and her worry over Jan making it on time, Elaine relaxed into her seat and took a deep breath. She glanced at her watch. Jan still had a few moments until the house lights dimmed, but there wasn't a thing Elaine could do to get her cousin there on time, and there was still an open seat next to her even as the show was about to begin, so she let it go.

Elaine focused straight ahead and located Avery near the right of the stage as the students found their seats. It was just like the rehearsal, except that there was a noticeably different electricity in the air. Both the audience and the orchestra knew this was a special event, and Elaine could practically feel the excitement.

The students played beautifully through several songs and Elaine allowed herself to get lost in the music. She had a lot to be thankful for, and her renewed faith in Nathan had her feeling particularly giddy. She was so caught up in the music that she startled a little when Jan, crouching down so as not to disturb the audience, found the seat next to her and sat down.

When Elaine looked over to smile at Jan, glad she'd made it before Avery's solo, she noticed that Jan's features looked strained and her shoulders were tense. She wished she could whisper and ask what was wrong, but there was an usher at the end of every few rows, and the one assigned to theirs did not look especially thrilled to be there. Either that or she took her job very seriously—maybe a little too seriously from the stern look on her face. She reminded Elaine of the way Jan described Mrs. Vennard, her strict fourth-grade teacher, but perhaps with fewer good intentions. Elaine made a mental note to catch the woman's eye and smile at her on her way out—sometimes a smiling face made a world of difference in someone's day, and she was feeling extra friendly that day. Maybe she could pass a little of it around.

The show continued and Elaine thought the students were doing a wonderful job, but all of that was shaded over by the anxious energy she could feel radiating from Jan. The second the show was over, she would ask her cousin what in the world was bothering her so much. Elaine didn't think the traffic, or being late, or having to search for a seat in the dark would rile her cousin that much, but she supposed that could be the cause.

She stopped thinking about it, though, when heard Avery begin to play her solo. Elaine held her breath and she could tell Jan was doing the same. Both made a sharp intake of breath as Avery slipped up on one note, then another, and Elaine's heart broke for the girl as she realized Avery might be making the same blunder she had before.

But then, something changed in Avery's demeanor midway through the piece—her shoulders went back, and her chin jutted out, and she seemed to talk herself into the confidence she'd shown when she'd played for the customers at Tea for Two the other day to such applause. Somehow, she turned it around, and managed to perform the rest of the solo to perfection. When Avery finished her solo, even though they were pretty far back, Elaine was almost certain the girl smiled as she joined in again with the rest of the instruments.

Elaine could hardly contain herself. It was all she could do not to stand up and clap right then and there, while the orchestra played on.

As her energy calmed, she recalled Jan's demeanor and looked over to see if her cousin seemed any more relaxed, but Jan was still in knots, and was now nearly sitting on the edge of the seat. Elaine caught Jan's eye and set her features in an expression that she hoped conveyed her confusion. Jan's eyes widened, and she tried desperately to mouth a few words to her cousin, but it was too dark for Elaine to read her lips.

After trying unsuccessfully to communicate for several minutes, Jan gave up. A moment later, she glanced over at the severe-looking usher—who had, unsurprisingly, been none too pleased to seat Jan when she'd come in late—and retrieved her purse from under the seat. Elaine watched as her cousin fished around inside the bag, then finally found her cell phone.

Oh dear, Elaine thought, this would really irk the usher. But there was absolutely nothing she could do, and a few seconds after she saw Jan typing away, the phone tucked near her side so as not to shine too brightly, Elaine felt her own phone buzz in her pocket.

She rolled her eyes and pulled it out as inconspicuously as she could manage, then turned it on, quickly changing the brightness settings to darken the screen as soon as she did so.

Elaine was waiting with bated breath for her eyes to adjust so she could find out what Jan was trying to text to her, when she felt a looming presence in the row behind her. The hairs on the back of her neck stood up as she turned around. There, only inches from her face, was the austere usher.

Uh-oh, Elaine thought. Jan had sure gotten them in trouble now.

The usher pointed to Elaine's phone, seemingly not even noticing Jan's, and motioned for her to put it away. It was plenty dark in the auditorium but Elaine was still sure she'd seen a beet-red glow rising up under the usher's skin. When she'd pocketed the phone and the woman seemed mildly quelled, Elaine poked Jan's thigh and glared at her cousin, feeling just like she had as a schoolgirl when, one time, another student had asked her a question and she'd gotten into trouble for talking when she'd tried to be helpful by answering. But Jan didn't seem fazed; in fact, she had the audacity to pull her phone out again and start tapping at the keyboard.

Elaine folded herself as far down in the seat as she could, hoping not to draw any more attention from the Usher of Doom, but luck wasn't on her side, and the second she tried to consult her own phone, fearing that something might really be wrong with Jan, the scary woman returned. This time, though, she wasn't to be trifled with, and she whispered harshly into Elaine's ear that if she did not put her phone away—*right this minute!*— she had every intention of ejecting Elaine from the theater and preventing her from ever returning for future events.

Feeling her cheeks burn like hot coals, Elaine acquiesced and turned off her phone before sliding it back into her purse, which she kicked further under the seat for good measure. Feeling cross, she folded her arms over her chest and glared at Jan, who stared straight ahead, ignoring her cousin.

When at last the concert concluded and the lights came back on, slowly increasing their brightness, Elaine fully intended to give Jan an earful about how unfair it was that she'd gotten into trouble and her cousin had not! She'd opened her mouth to begin a loudly whispered lecture when Jan surprised her by grabbing her arm and dragging her out into the foyer, not even waiting to congratulate Avery.

"Listen, Elaine," she said, her words spilling out rapidly, "I've got to tell you something important."

Elaine was still peeved. "It'd better be," she said, "because you nearly got me kicked out back there and—"

Jan held up a hand to quiet her. "I'm sorry about that—really, I am—but we don't have time to talk about it now."

"All right, but you've got to tell me what is going on," Elaine said.

Jan responded by putting a hand on Elaine's shoulder to lead her out of the auditorium.

"Wait!" Elaine cried out, planting her feet. "We've got to say hello to Avery and I wanted to stop and get her some flowers." She pointed at a little stand near the front entrance.

Jan shook her head. "We don't have time," she said adamantly.

"All right," Elaine said, sounding as stern to her own ears as the usher had before. "That's enough. I'm not moving from this spot"—she pointed to her feet—"until you tell me precisely what is going on with you."

CHAPTER TWENTY

J an seemed frustrated at delaying another second, but she
closed her eyes and said, "Okay, okay. I was going to wait
until we got there so we didn't waste time, but—"

"Got where?" Elaine asked.

"That's what I'm trying to tell you," Jan said on an exasper-
ated release of breath. "Remember when I called those moving
guys that left the business card? I left a few messages for them
to return my call, under the pretense of telling them they won
the free pastry contest."

Elaine nodded.

"Right, well, I got a call back right before you left the house.
That's why I stayed behind and was running so late."

"What did they say that has you in such a state?" Elaine
asked, her worry increasing by the minute.

"The mover I spoke with recalls a job the night the statue
went missing. He said he and his buddy moved a massive, heavy
object matching my description of the statue. He says they even
needed straps to lift it because it was so heavy."

Elaine nodded rapidly.

"The person who hired the movers doubled the usual rate to move the object back to his family home in the middle of the night." She paused as the information sunk in. "And here's the most interesting part," Jan continued. "That person went by the name of Jonathan Frost."

Elaine frowned. "But Jonathan Frost is dead," she said.

Jan nodded, her lips pursed. "That's right," she said. "I think the person was using Frost as an assumed name to hide his real identity when he had them move the stolen statue."

"Where are we going?" Elaine asked as Jan practically dragged her from the auditorium. "My car is still parked here."

"It will have to wait," Jan said as they got into her Toyota. "We've got to get to this Frost person's house as quickly as possible."

"Wait, what?" Elaine asked, confused.

Jan started up the car and pulled on her seat belt, glancing in the rearview mirror before she pulled out onto the highway. "The movers were kind enough to give me Jonathan Frost's address so that I can send the guy free pastries to thank him for bringing business to town," Jan said, briefly removing her hands from the steering wheel to put air quotes around the false name. She caught Elaine's skeptical look. "I know it's flimsy, but they gave it to me anyway. I don't know who took the statue yet, but I have a pretty good idea we'll find it when we get to that house."

Elaine sat back in her seat and watched the dark sky outside her passenger-side window, working to make sense of what Jan was saying. She thought back over all the facts they had so far, and some of the other things that had been bothering her because they seemed important but out of place.

Eventually her thoughts traveled back to the night before, when she and Nathan had stopped at the library on the way back to Lancaster. Something had been bugging her about that malfunctioning key, and as her mind churned, she began to put the pieces together.

"Oh my goodness," she said, gripping the seat. "I think I know who took the statue."

"You do?" Jan asked, swerving just slightly before regaining control of the car.

"It has to be Adam Watkins." Elaine continued after Jan gave an unsure look. "Think about it. It has to be Watkins. He's been studying the history of the statue for decades, and he's probably built up enough connections to have been able to follow its whereabouts all this time. He's got loads of people listed at the back of that book of his."

Jan still looked unconvinced, but Elaine had her attention.

"Also, Nathan told me something very interesting on our date the other night. If you can believe it, Watkins has befriended him and has played a game of racquetball with Nathan. They've even scheduled another for this weekend, following the fund-raiser—if we have it."

"I'm listening," Jan said.

"Here's the weird part," Elaine continued, growing more and more certain of Watkins's guilt as she laid out all she knew. "Nathan and I tried to drop off a basket of stuff at the library last night. Priscilla had given him keys in case he needed to move the statue into the storage room when she wasn't there. But when we tried it in the lock, the key didn't work."

"I'm not sure I see where this is going," Jan said.

"I think that, somehow, Watkins found out about the statue being willed to the town of Lancaster, and discovered that it was placed in Nathan's care and that Nathan had library keys—maybe by following him, or maybe he saw Priscilla hand Nathan the keys one day when the library was open because, according to both Rose and Priscilla, he was in there a lot. I don't know for sure. But I believe Watkins stole the real library key from Nathan, and replaced it with a decoy key."

Jan's eyes were wide as she stared at the road. "It does make sense," she said. "It all makes sense, actually. And I bet that Watkins bought the mannequin from Harrison as a ruse, so that if anyone saw him in the shop, or saw his truck outside the day he stole the lumberjack mannequin, he would have an alibi, and Harrison would have the receipt to back him up."

Elaine nodded emphatically. "Yes! I hadn't even thought of that yet, but you're right. It absolutely adds up."

"We're not too far out," Jan said, glancing quickly at the map app on her phone, into which she'd punched the address the movers had given her. "I think it would be a good idea to call Trooper Benson and let him know what we're up to, in case we meet with any trouble."

"This time," Elaine said, chuckling, "I wholeheartedly agree."

She called Dan as Jan continued to drive, and when he picked up on the second ring, Elaine explained herself rapidly. Dan was skeptical at first, but when she told him what she and Jan had just worked out, he was convinced enough to drop what he was doing and hop in his SUV.

"I'll be there as soon as I can," he said into the phone. "Don't do anything reckless, you hear?"

"I promise," Elaine said. "We're only going to see where the house is and take a look around. We won't talk to anyone or get into any trouble."

"Okay," Dan said, not sounding convinced. "See you soon."

A few moments later, Jan pulled onto a quiet street lined on either side with bare trees. It looked like any other street, and Jan scanned the numbers on either side of the road until she found the one she wanted. "That's it," she said, but kept going until she'd moved a few homes down, then made a U-turn and parked her Camry on the street.

"Good thinking," Elaine said. "But it's too bad I didn't bring my binoculars."

Jan grinned and pulled the pair out of her purse. "It's okay," she said. "I brought a pair of my own. Just in case." She winked.

"What do we do now?" Elaine asked.

Jan turned in her seat. "Let's just keep an eye on things until Trooper Benson gets here. We can't get into the house anyway, so we might as well just sit tight and wait."

They did just that for a little while, both glancing at their watches frequently, guessing how far out Dan might be, when suddenly Elaine saw movement at the address Jan had been given. "I think I see something," she said. "Look, over at the house."

Jan held the binoculars up to her eyes. "It's a taxi," she said, craning her neck closer to the window. "I think it's one of those that bring you from your house to the airport and vice versa."

They watched in silence as an elderly woman got out of the car and then went around to the trunk. The taxi driver helped her get her bags out before driving away. The woman—whom Elaine guessed must have been in her eighties—had just turned to walk toward the house when she spotted Elaine and Jan in the car, the binoculars still plastered to Jan's face. She started heading toward them.

"Oh no!" Jan said. "I think she saw me."

Jan hunkered down in the seat, but it was too late. They'd been caught. When the woman arrived at their car, she began knocking hard on the window, making fervent hand motions for Elaine to open the window—now!

Elaine obliged and pushed the button, letting the window slide down into her door, trying as it did to think of something to say that could plausibly explain their presence. "Hello," she said, making her voice sound as cheerful as possible. "Can I help you?"

The woman put her hands on her hips and glared into Jan's car. "I certainly hope so," she said. "You can start by explaining what you're doing here and why you're staring at my house with those things." She pointed a thin finger at the binoculars, which Jan had removed and placed on the floor near her feet to try to hide them, evidently not well enough.

"Oh," Jan said. "Well..."

Elaine sighed as Jan tried unsuccessfully to explain. Finally, Jan gave up and glanced pleadingly at her cousin.

The truth was always the best option, Elaine thought.

"It's a long story—," she began, but the woman interrupted her.

"I'm not sure I care to hear it," the woman shouted, her pale skin turning a bright shade of red. "I'd rather you just stop staring at my house and get off this street before I call the police."

It was at that exact moment that Dan turned the corner onto the street, police lights flashing from the top of his SUV. He spotted Jan's car and parked next to her before getting out quickly.

"What's going on?" he asked, looking accusingly at Jan and Elaine. "I thought I told you to wait until I got here and to stay out of trouble."

The old woman was obviously so angry now that Elaine would not have been the least bit amazed to see steam rising from her ears.

"All right, that's it!" she shouted. "I demand to know what's going on this instant!"

Dan turned from Jan and Elaine, who were still in the car, and waved his hands up and down, palms down, to try and calm the woman. Briefly, and with far more patience than Elaine could have mustered, he started to explain the situation. The woman stood staring at him in disbelief.

"May I ask your name?" he asked before introducing himself.

The woman glared at him but then rolled her eyes and gave in. "Oh, okay. I'm Stephanie Watkins, if you must know."

"Are you any relation to a Professor Adam Watkins?" Dan asked.

"Why, yes," she answered. "That's my son."

Dan told her what he suspected and asked politely if he might see into her garage, and was obviously relieved when she didn't ask to see a warrant.

Jan and Elaine got out of the car, and as they walked to the house, Mrs. Watkins, still in shock, explained that she had in fact noticed some recent behavior changes in Adam—he'd become more and more obsessed with his work and kept going on tirades about a statue that had been "given to the wrong person" and that "needed to be returned to its rightful place where the author had worked"—and that she'd been concerned. However, she'd previously scheduled a lengthy vacation overseas, and had planned to talk with Adam when she returned.

When they got to Mrs. Watkins's home, she obligingly opened the garage, and neither Jan, Elaine, nor Dan were surprised to see the famed bronze likeness of Phillip Camden right there in the garage, staring back at them.

Stephanie Watkins gasped. "I have no idea what that's doing in here," she said. "You've got to believe me."

"No one suspects you of any crime," Dan said placatingly.

"While I was on vacation, I asked him to move some things for me, like my old wedding gown and a few other things, into a storage unit," Stephanie explained. "I didn't know he'd replace them with this."

Jan and Elaine exchanged a knowing glance.

"I just can't believe that my son did this," Stephanie said sadly.

Elaine reached over to pat her shoulder. "It's not your fault," she said. "It sounds like he just got too deep into his work, and he believed that the statue truly was in the wrong place."

Stephanie nodded. "Those Camden books meant so much to him growing up. His father was absent a lot for work, and I think Adam just wanted something to make him feel better. He used to take medication for his…problems…but, looking back, I suspect he may have gone off them some time ago, when that book of his was released."

Elaine nodded, sad to hear that Adam's love of Phillip Camden's books had evolved into an unhealthy obsession, and that his mental health had suffered for it.

As Jan and Elaine listened to Mrs. Watkins's sad story, Dan called a local deputy in Waterville to ask that she detain Adam at the Corinth Hotel until he could get over there to make an arrest. Dan stayed on the phone with her, but when the deputy arrived at the Corinth, Watkins was nowhere to be found. Dan was about to put out an APB when they all heard a noise and turned to see Adam standing in the doorway.

"What's going on here?" he shouted.

Dan hung up his phone and moved slowly toward Adam, who looked as though he'd been up all night. His eyes were bloodshot, his hair wild, and his clothes disheveled. He looked crazed.

As Dan approached and explained that he was under arrest and informed him of his rights, Adam began a rant about how the statue's rightful place was in Augusta.

"Phillip Camden was the greatest author who ever lived," he spat, as Dan calmly clicked handcuffs shut around his wrists. "Camden spent his last years working as a professor at the University of Maine campus," he said, "where *I* happen to work. The statue belongs there, rather than in Lancaster. I only needed to keep it until I had a chance to challenge Frost's will. He obviously didn't know what a big mistake he was making."

Dan placed a hand on Adam's shoulder and led him out of the garage.

"Lancaster is only significant because that's where Camden was born!" Adam continued to yell. "Any scholar worth his salt knows that he only wrote a small portion of his work there. It's not nearly as important as where he worked and taught. We deserve to have that statue at *my* university."

Elaine noticed that Adam left out the fact that the work Camden created in Lancaster was by far his most famous, and that Camden's love for the small, quiet town was evident in those works.

"Okay. That ought to do," Dan said quietly.

Adam raved on and on, and Dan worked to get him into his truck before rushing back to hand Stephanie his card, asking her to contact him to give a statement. Elaine and Jan did their best to comfort Adam's distraught mother, offering to call later and check in with her, before they headed home.

It was only after they had stopped by Brian's house to belatedly congratulate Avery on her performance and returned home, and Dan too had made it back to Lancaster, that they learned the rest of Adam's story. Dan came by the tearoom later that night and talked to them both.

Apparently, Adam had befriended Nathan under the guise of wanting a good racquetball game, after hanging out at the library and figuring out that Nathan had become the statue's caretaker and that it was in his safekeeping. Adam had indeed seen Priscilla handing him a an extra set of keys to the library, and during the racquetball game a couple weeks ago, Adam took Nathan's key and replaced it with a decoy. After observing Priscilla's daily movements for a while, he then used the key to get into the library and shut down the computer system.

He intended to switch the keys back after using the library key to let the movers in to transport the statue from the storage room where Nathan had stowed it, but he did not have a chance to meet with Nathan again for their second racquetball game. Adam also told Trooper Benson that he'd hired the movers to pick up the statue from the library and take it to his mother's home in Augusta, knowing that his mother would not be home for a few weeks and no one was likely to find it. He also revealed his intent to anonymously place the statue on the university campus there.

When Dan finished telling them the details of what had happened, he thanked them. "Once again, you two have been a huge help. We were at a loss there for a while, and I didn't think we'd ever solve this case."

"Well, we had a good reason to get involved," Elaine said, thinking of Nathan, who had been ecstatic when she'd told him about Watkins's arrest, and that there was no reason not to think the statue would be returned in time for the fund-raiser that weekend.

"And I bet I know a few movers who would be willing to help get the statue back to Lancaster!" Jan said.

CHAPTER TWENTY-ONE

The following Saturday marked the arrival of the fund-raiser they'd all been anticipating. Up until now, Elaine thought, it had been mostly with apprehension. But when the day came, Nathan picked up Elaine and Jan on foot and, bundled up against the cold air, they walked happily across Main Street to the library.

"Do you think it'll get there in time?" Elaine asked Jan, who was walking beside her. She turned to see her cousin's face.

"It'll be a close one," Jan responded. "I asked those movers to come as soon as Dan took all the prints and cleared the statue from evidence, so I hope they'll make it for the scheduled unveiling."

"Me too," Elaine said. "I think the board members—not to mention the whole town of Lancaster—all deserve to see it in its proper place."

"I'm so relieved," Nathan said. "I knew how it looked when everyone thought I had something to do with the statue's theft, and I couldn't stomach the thought of people assuming I was a thief."

Elaine reached over to where his hand rested at his side and grasped it. "I don't think anyone truly believed you had anything to do with it," she said.

"I'm not so sure. I think Priscilla regretted giving me the keys to the library," he said.

"Well, it all worked out okay in the end, didn't it?" Jan pointed out.

Elaine frowned, her thoughts turning to another mother whose day most likely wasn't going as well as her own. "Not for Mrs. Watkins," she said sadly.

Jan made a soft noise of agreement. "You're right," she said. "I hope she'll find peace, and that Adam will receive the help he needs to start the journey to getting better."

"Me too," Elaine said. "It must have been so hard for her to find out that her son had planned and executed a crime. I can't imagine how she must be feeling right now."

"I think she probably feels like it's somehow her fault," Jan mused. "I don't think any mother can help feeling that way when something like that happens with a child."

Elaine nodded. "That's so true. But what happened to Adam is not her fault, and I intend to keep her in my prayers."

"Me too," Jan added, and Nathan did the same.

It was as beautiful a day as one could ask for in the middle of a Maine winter. It was eminently clear that a big celebration was going on inside the library. Elaine just stood there, enjoying the rays of sun that had slipped through the clouds, and took it all in. Colorful streamers had been strung up across the library's entrance, and its pretty bricks were basking in the little bit of sun. Near the front of the building, patio heaters had been set up so people could stay warm enough while viewing the statue, and there was a large area cordoned off where it was meant to stand once the movers arrived. Elaine glanced at her watch, praying that they made it there on time.

"I'm off," Nathan said before kissing Elaine's cheek. "I've got to go speak with Priscilla."

Elaine smiled up into his blue eyes, thankful that he once again wore a smile on his handsome face. She'd missed it there for a while.

She and Jan headed inside the library to explore. Space had been cleared and there were little tables set up every-where, with local crafters selling their creations. Elaine spot-ted everything from homemade candles to beautifully carved old-fashioned wooden toys. And on every breath of air she smelled a new, delicious food scent. There was a stand selling freshly baked loaves of artisan bread, locally aged cheeses, and even candy apples.

"All of this looks so good," Jan said as they strolled past the tables, smiling and waving at the proprietors. It was a tight squeeze inside the building, but everyone mulled about hap-pily, glad for the warmth of close quarters.

"It does," Elaine said. "I'm glad we didn't eat breakfast so we can pick something to enjoy."

In addition to the fee to participate, each of the artisans present promised to voluntarily donate twenty percent of their proceeds for the day to the library, so Elaine and Jan had been sure to grab cash before leaving the house.

"I don't need too much coaxing to spend money on won-derful food," Jan said, smiling, "but it just sweetens the deal to know that it's for such a good cause. Besides, I have some news to celebrate."

Elaine turned to look at her cousin, eyes wide. "Well, don't keep me in suspense. What is it?"

Jan's eyes sparkled. "Bob is coming home!"

"That's wonderful!" Elaine said. "I'm so glad to hear it. But why didn't you tell me sooner?"

"Bob asked me to keep mum until he'd finalized the paperwork, which he has done now. It's been so hard not knowing whether he would ever return to Lancaster. But he called and said that our relationship is more important than the job and that the kind of work he's doing in Baltimore would serve smaller communities too, like here in the central Maine area. He's decided to open his own law firm."

"Wow!" Elaine exclaimed. "What a change of heart."

"He said life is too short and he didn't want to waste another minute without me to share it with," Jan explained, smiling warmly.

"So, when's the big day?" Elaine asked.

"In just a few weeks, if you can believe it," Jan answered. "Bob's coming back to get things started here next week, but he'll have to make a few trips back and forth to get everything moved and sorted out."

"I'm so happy for you, Jan," Elaine said, squeezing her cousin's shoulder before they walked on. After that, they wandered around, enjoying each other's company and trying to decide what to eat.

"Everything looks amazing. I don't know what to pick," Jan said, echoing Elaine's earlier thoughts.

"How about a kolache from that table over there?" Elaine suggested, pointing across the way.

"Sounds amazing," Jan agreed. "I'm in."

They walked across the narrow space and approached the vendor they'd chosen. Elaine ordered an egg and cheese kolache and Jan picked sausage and egg.

"How about we add a raspberry one for dessert?" Jan suggested.

"You don't have to ask me twice," Elaine agreed, grinning at the thought.

They paid for their purchases and continued walking as they ate. The first bite of soft bread was heavenly, and it just got better on the next when Elaine reached the fluffy scrambled eggs and melted cheddar inside. By the time they were finished, Jan was promising to go back and ask for the recipes, and Elaine was regretting not getting a second. Feeling full and happy, they headed over to where Rose and Archie were running Tea for Two's little table.

"Hey," Rose whispered loudly to Archie as the two women approached. "Those ladies look a little familiar."

Archie rolled his eyes and they all laughed.

"How's it going here, you two?" Jan asked.

"It's going well," Rose said. "We've had a crazy turnout so far, and the day's only just begun."

Elaine admired the spread that Rose and Jan had gotten up early to make while she and Archie had spent the morning brewing as much tea as their large metal containers would hold. She was glad that she and Jan had decided to pay Rose and Archie time and a half for their shift that day, since the pink glow in Rose's cheeks suggested they'd been working extra hard.

They all visited for a bit, as the crowd began to rapidly increase until almost every table had an astonishingly long line of people wanting to buy things. It was a great turnout, Elaine thought, so pleased that everything had been cleared up with Adam Watkins and the police so Nathan could enjoy the day he'd worked so hard to achieve.

She couldn't see out of the library's front window for the crowd, but she hoped the statue had already arrived and was waiting to be unveiled—this time, hopefully, with a different outcome.

Elaine was lost in her thoughts as Archie, Rose, and Jan chattered around her when she saw Geraldine approach the table, accompanied by Archie's wife, Gloria.

"Good morning," they all said to the two women as they greeted them in return.

"This is just…"

"Well,…"

Geraldine and Gloria laughed and Archie came out from behind the table to give them both a big hug.

"Did you tell them the news?" Geraldine asked Archie, her features glowing as she stared up into his face—a face that, Elaine thought, standing there—was not unlike her own.

Archie shook his head. "I was waiting until you got here so we could tell them together."

All eyes were on the two of them as they stayed quiet.

"Tell us what?" Jan finally asked, joyful anticipation in her voice.

"We got the results back from the DNA tests," Archie said, beaming, "and...it's almost certain that Geraldine and I are related!"

There were loud gasps of surprise all around, so much that they drew attention from the nearby booths, but they were too excited to care.

"We're likely half brother and sister," Geraldine added, her face lighting up with joy.

"Oh, that's wonderful," Elaine said, her heart swelling for the two of them. "You're family!"

"It would seem so," Archie said, grinning.

"We just knew there was something there," Geraldine said, "but I think we hadn't yet worked up the courage to really do something about it."

"Aren't you glad you finally did?" Jan asked, clasping her hands together.

"Absolutely," Archie and Geraldine said at the same time, laughing. "It's so exciting to have found each other," Geraldine said. "And not only a brother, but a sister too," she added, linking her arm with Gloria's.

"But now the real work begins," Archie said, sharing a look with his newfound sister.

"Yes, now we have to continue looking into my adoption, and find out what really happened to our father and to Geraldine's mum," Archie said.

"You've got each other now, though," Elaine said, "so you can continue the journey together."

The six of them spent a little more time together and then Jan looked at her watch, announcing that they all needed to get outside to the front of the library fast.

They began making their way through the doors and toward one of the patio heaters, the crowd becoming so thick that they were shoulder to shoulder with the people around them. Elaine nearly shouted with glee when she caught sight of a giant object hidden beneath a velvet cover, and saw Nathan climb up onto the stage to take his place at the microphone.

She listened intently as Nathan gave a similar speech to the one he'd given at the board meeting. She prayed fervently that this time, it would be the prelude to something wonderful. Glancing around, she thanked God for the many blessings in her life—especially for the kindhearted people surrounding her, all of whom she now considered family. And when she heard those words again...

"Finally," Nathan said, flashing that smile that so warmed Elaine's heart, "we've come to the moment you've all been waiting for."

And with that, the cover was lifted from the statue to much applause, and there was Phillip Camden, whose smile seemed to wish them all a very happy ending indeed.

ABOUT THE AUTHOR

A my Woods is the coauthor (with Kristin Eckhardt) of *O Christmas Tea*, the sixth volume in Guideposts' Tearoom Mysteries series, as well as several other books. She was a reader before she ever dreamed of becoming a writer, and still relishes curling up with a new book by a favorite author more than just about anything else. She and her husband of a decade make their home in Central Texas with their too-smart-for-her-own-good rescue dog.

From the Tea for Two Kitchen
Rose's Macarons

While they are spelled similarly, macaroons and macarons (mac-uh-ROHNs) are two quite different cookies. Macarons are light-as-a-feather sandwich cookies, often quite colorful, while macaroons are usually golden-tan in color and made with coconut. Macarons can be a challenge, but here is an easy-to-make version for you to try.

1¼ cups almond meal or almond flour

1¾ cups confectioner's sugar

¼ teaspoon salt

4 large egg whites

½ cup granulated sugar

¼ teaspoon almond extract

Optional: food coloring of your choice (macarons typically are made in pastel colors such as mint green, baby blue, or pink)

Strained jam or other desired filling

Whisk almond meal or almond flour, confectioner's sugar, and salt together, then sift over a large bowl. In a separate bowl, use a hand mixer to beat egg whites until they become frothy (about one to two minutes) and peaked. Add granulated sugar (slowly) and almond extract. Beat until shiny medium peaks form (about three to five minutes). Gently fold egg whites into the almond mixture until just combined. (If using food coloring, add it as you fold the egg whites in, using just a drop at a time until the desired light pastel hue is achieved.) Using a spatula, vigorously mix until the mixture sinks easily into a smooth mass, with a honey-like consistency. Transfer the mixture to a pastry bag and cut approximately one-half inch off of the bag's tip.

Line cookie sheets with parchment paper, then pipe mixture onto the parchment in one-inch rounds approximately 1 inch apart. Allow to dry for thirty to ninety minutes, or until the tops are dry and firm. Preheat oven to 350 degrees and bake one sheet at a time in your preheated oven for approximately fourteen minutes, rotating the sheet pan once midway.

Allow macarons to cool completely on wire racks, then fill and sandwich cookies together. Makes twenty-four to twenty-eight sandwich cookies.

READ ON FOR AN EXCITING SNEAK PEEK
INTO THE NEXT VOLUME OF TEAROOM MYSTERIES!

Whispers from the Past
BY ANNE MARIE RODGERS

Tea for Two was slow on the last Friday in March. So slow, in fact, that right after lunch there wasn't a single patron in the lovely old restored Victorian on the shore of Chickadee Lake in central Maine.

The two elegant rooms where Jan Blake and Elaine Cook served tea and tasty pastries stood empty. The cousins, however, were in high gear as they prepared to leave for the weekend, something they had never done at the same time before.

Jan carried a large sealed baggie with tissue-thin sheets of phyllo dough to the refrigerator and carefully laid them flat on a cookie sheet in the freezer. For Monday's daily special, she planned to bake apple strudel using phyllo dough. She would not have time to make the dough this weekend, so she'd rolled it and placed it between layers of waxed paper for quick thawing.

She glanced out the window of the back door at Chickadee Lake, where patches of dark water were beginning to show as the deep freeze of winter receded. Some years the lake ice stayed thick much longer, but it hadn't been as cold as long this year. The ice fishing season was drawing to a close as the ice became unstable, and all of the ice shanties that had dotted the flat surface of the lake had been removed. It was a good thing too. She recalled an incident last week when someone drove a truck onto the ice. It slowly began to sink as the day passed, and the owner had been forced to call for a tow from shore before the lake swallowed his truck completely.

Walking into the dining room, she glanced at the time. "It's almost three, and we need to leave in about forty-five minutes," she said to her cousin Elaine, who also was the co-owner of their home and business.

Elaine's mother, Virginia Willard, had invited both Elaine and Jan to attend a mother-daughter retreat for the coming weekend at a lovely old hotel close to the other end of Chickadee Lake. Virginia and many of her high school friends who belonged to the same chapter of her service guild, Delta, would be gathering to revisit their school days together with their family members. Elaine's daughter, Sasha, had flown in from Colorado and was to join them as well. The theme was the Victorian Era, and the program chair had asked the cousins to serve and hold a short talk on Victorian tea rituals during the Sunday-morning break.

Jan had been looking forward to the weekend for some time. She still was. Except that Bob Claybrook, her beau, had just returned to Maine from Baltimore after deciding that it was too difficult to make their relationship work long distance. It gave her a warm glow to hear him say that she was more important to him than his job in the mid-Atlantic region. Additionally, he seemed excited about his plans to open his own local law firm, and she was sorry that she would be gone all weekend just when they were weaving the threads of their relationship into a new and stronger emotional fabric.

Maybe, she thought, she could sneak away for a short time during the retreat and spend a little time with him. She felt positively adolescent about her desire to be with him as much as possible. Grinning at herself, she refocused on her task.

The antique cherry table was covered with an assortment of items Jan and Elaine would need for their talk, and Jan mentally reviewed all the items on its surface to ensure they hadn't forgotten anything. "What else do we need to pack?"

Elaine screwed up her face as she registered Jan's question. "I wish the tea had arrived," she said, frowning. They had ordered from a company they hadn't used before. "Maybe I shouldn't have taken a chance with a new vendor, since we need it for a specific event."

The tea, Jan knew, was called Friendship and Memories. They both had thought it was a perfect fit for the weekend. The women in Virginia's group had been friends now for roughly sixty years, and the tea's name had been so evocative Elaine had not been able to resist it.

"Oh, but it will be so perfect. Have you tried tracking it online?" Jan asked.

"Not yet. I need to go do that right now," Elaine said.

"If it doesn't arrive until tomorrow, one of us can run home and get it," Jan assured her. "Thank goodness this retreat is so close to Tea for Two."

Elaine hitched a thumb over her shoulder. "I'll go check on the status of the delivery."

Jan nodded. "And I'll get this stuff packed up."

As Elaine left the room, Archie Bentham, the Englishman who worked for them, entered. "Need some help?" he asked Jan in his cultured British accent. "I'm bored to tears. If we don't get more customers today, I may be reduced to dusting." Archie was a retired expat from the UK who had applied for work at the tearoom to keep himself busy, but more importantly, because he loved tea. Polished and well-traveled, Archie had become an indispensable member of their little team.

"I'd love some help. We need to get all this into Elaine's car," Jan said, indicating the piles of intricately folded cloth napkins, the stacks of vintage teapots, cups, saucers, sugars and creamers, the boxes of sweeteners, and jars of honey. "Did you hear Elaine say the tea she was expecting for this weekend hasn't arrived yet? If it shows up after we leave—"

"If it shows up later, I'll be happy to run it over," Archie said. "It's not as if you're heading off to Siberia."

"Bite your tongue," Jan said with a grin. "I hope we are done with those kinds of temperatures for this year. I'm ready for spring."

Archie chuckled. "Bit early for that. There's nothing on the radar for the next week, but you know we're going to get snow a couple more times, and at least one of those will be a doozy."

"As long as it melts quickly, I can stand it," Jan said.

The sound of the house telephone interrupted their casual banter. Jan set down the teacup she was about to place into a small compartment in the divided dishware box she'd put together. "I'll get that." Heading into the foyer, she crossed to the table that held the house telephone in its cradle. Lifting the handset, she said, "Hello?"

"Hello, Jan, it's Gloria. Is Archie close by? I tried his cell phone, but he didn't pick up."

Jan already had recognized the voice of Archie's wife. There was an odd note in her voice, perhaps one of urgency. "Hi, Gloria. He probably left it in the kitchen on vibrate. I don't believe he keeps it with him when he's working. I'll get him for you. Hold on."

After returning to the dining room, Jan quickly sent Archie to the foyer when he confirmed that, as she'd suspected, he didn't have his cell phone in his pocket. She resisted the urge to follow him to see what was going on. It might be human to be curious, but it was bad manners to eavesdrop, she reminded herself.

She didn't have to wait long to have her curiosity satisfied. Mere moments later, Archie's hurried footsteps could be heard coming back to the dining room. "Do you mind if I take a few minutes?" he asked. "Rose says she can handle things temporarily. Something's come up." Rose, their other employee, was still in one of the parlors restocking clean linen.

Jan was alarmed. "Go, go," she said, making shooing motions. "Is Gloria okay?"

"Oh, it's nothing like that." Archie looked sheepish, but there was no mistaking the excitement in his voice. "No real emergency. It's just that we finally heard from the art authenticator. They've confirmed that your painting is, indeed, one of my father's works. And it seems the fellow's found some sort of note tucked in between the painting and the frame. He's got some questions for me."

Jan's eyes widened. "So he believes it's original?"

"Yes, and he told Gloria he believed the note dates to the time the painting was done," Archie said.

Jan could hear the exhilaration rising in her voice "Maybe it's something your father wrote! You'd better call him right now."

Archie shrugged, trying to appear calm, although she could tell it was an effort. "I have to think that's a possibility at least. If it's handwritten, I might recognize his handwriting. Or at least be able to compare it to other things that were written by him."

"How exciting!"

"What's exciting?" Elaine stepped back into the room from her office.

As Archie left the room, Jan told Elaine about the telephone call. "Oh, it would be wonderful if it helped Archie learn more about his father," Elaine said. "Or if he finds confirmation from him that he and Geraldine are sister and brother."

"I know." Jan nodded. "So what did you find out about the tea?"

Elaine sighed. "The shipping order says it was delivered yesterday."

"It was not." Jan was indignant.

"That's what I said. I e-mailed the company and asked them to track it from their end, since I didn't receive it. Unless I hear from them in the next half hour or so, I'll just have to stay on top of it and keep checking my e-mail after we get to the retreat."

Jan frowned. "Well, that's frustrating."

"Very," Elaine agreed. "I'm hoping we can straighten it out. If it arrives tomorrow, Archie or Rose can bring it over."

"Archie already volunteered to run it by," Jan assured her.

They had debated about the wisdom of them both leaving the tearoom on a Saturday, but Archie and Rose had assured them that they could handle it for one day. Elaine and Jan had accepted Virginia's invitation, knowing that the tearoom would be in good hands.

Jan's parents were both deceased, so when Virginia had told her fondly that "I consider you an honorary daughter, and I'd be delighted if you could attend," Jan had gotten a little teary for a moment.

Each of them had a small wheeled suitcase packed and waiting in the front hall. A garment bag held two of the Victorian-era costumes they wore for special days at the tearoom; they would don those before their presentation on Sunday. A small, orderly stack of supplies also waited to one side.

In addition, Jan had two boxes containing the ingredients for a "friendship bread" she intended to make in the hotel's kitchen to be served with the tea. As soon as they got the rest of the dishware packed, they would be ready to go.

"I apologize for making this a working weekend," Elaine said. "When I said we'd give a tea presentation, I wasn't thinking about you having to make the friendship bread."

"It's no problem," Jan said. "I called over on Thursday and the kitchen manager said I could use their ovens either Saturday evening or before they begin their breakfast preparations Sunday morning."

"When are you going to do it?"

"I'm not sure yet," Jan said. "I wanted to take a look at the schedule and see when might be the best time."

When they were finished packing the dishes and other things they needed, Elaine got her keys, and soon the cousins began loading their supplies and personal luggage into her Chevy Malibu. Earl Grey, the long-haired "stray" cat who loved to sleep on their back porch, came around the corner of the house to say his farewells. He consented to petting and cuddles from both women before extracting himself to return to his snooze.

Fortunately, the weather had cooperated for the folks who would be traveling some distance to attend the retreat. Both cousins luxuriated in the mid-fifties temperature, which felt positively balmy compared to the below-zero chill in which they had been frozen last week.

Elaine had just closed the trunk and started up the steps to get her handbag when Archie stepped out the door.

"What's the scoop?" she called.

"I don't know," he said. "I tried to call him back but the line was busy twice, and then the third time I had to leave a message. Did you still need me to help you pack?"

The cousins chuckled. "No," Jan said, "we took care of it. We're taking off now, so thank you again for standing in for us tomorrow."

"You're most welcome," Archie said. "And best wishes with your presentation on Sunday. I'll let you know when the tea shipment arrives and bring it over as soon as Rose and I get things in order after closing." He greeted four women who were coming up the sidewalk to the front porch. "Hello, ladies. Welcome to Tea for Two. Please come in."

"Great," Elaine said. "We'll see you then. Thanks, Archie."

After adding a few last-minute items, the cousins climbed into Elaine's car, and she pulled the sedan onto Main Street. After a few hundred yards, she took the eastern side of Cottage Road around the lake toward the small town of Penzance, roughly three miles away at the far end of the lake. Just outside the Penzance town limits lay their destination, the Whisperwood Hotel.

It took less than fifteen minutes to travel to the hotel.

"I hope it's as pretty inside as it is outside," said Jan as Elaine pulled into the circle that fronted the sixty-odd-room building. "I've always thought this place was so picturesque and lovely, but I've never stayed here. This will be a treat."

"It would have been more of a treat thirty years ago," Elaine pointed out. "It's a little run-down now."

"I remember coming to the dining room for a birthday party once when I was a child," Jan said. "It was quite charming, and dozens of wealthy summer people stayed here back then."

The Whisperwood was three stories high, with a wide, columned front porch where inviting rocking chairs waited. Shallow stone steps led up to the porch. Painted a soft sky blue with white trim, the main building put one in mind of a wedding cake. At one side, a rectangular addition with a handicapped ramp led into the dining room, giving guests in wheelchairs or with rolling luggage easier access to the main porch, from which they could access the front entry. Jan had attended a wedding reception and a retirement dinner in the restaurant more recently, which she estimated seated about a hundred and fifty people when all the partitions were opened.

East Cottage Road passed between the lake and the hotel, so all the "best" rooms at the front of the historic structure had a lake view. Elaine was right about its faded, shabby appearance. Built in 1898, the hotel had been a thriving, bustling tourist destination for many, many summers, but in the last thirty years, business had fallen off. Both cousins could remember the hordes of summer tourists who hiked and swam, canoed on the lake, and browsed through little shops in Penzance and Lancaster. Many of the families had come back year after year; the "regulars," locals had called them.

Elaine put the car in park. "Why don't we just unload our personal stuff for the moment? We can ask at the desk where they'd like us to bring our supplies for the Sunday presentation."

"Okay." Jan gave her a thumbs-up and climbed from the passenger seat. Elaine popped the trunk and came to help her, and the cousins efficiently unloaded their suitcases and costumes onto the sidewalk in front of the steps.

"Back in a minute," Elaine said. After moving the car to a nearby parking lot, she returned, and the cousins gathered their belongings and headed up the steps to the deep-red front door.

Inside, the lobby was filled with quaint groupings of floral-upholstered chairs and loveseats, paintings of the lake and the hotel from yesteryear, and several large and thriving potted plants. The check-in desk was charming, composed of age-darkened wooden panels with three Tiffany-style glass hanging lights overhead featuring swooping dragonflies. Behind the desk hung an antique key rack containing large numbered keys.

Women clogged the room in groups, most with pieces of luggage and handbags the size of small suitcases. The noise level was at a high decibel, a distinct cacophony of female voices punctuated by the occasional shriek as old friends found each other in the crowd.

"... going to be a great-grandma! Can you believe it?" A tall woman grinned, looking thrilled.

A graying blonde rushed across the room and embraced a shorter woman with flame-red curls. "CeeCee! It's so wonderful..."

The gabble of excited voices was deafening.

Blazing a trail to the desk, Jan and Elaine waited to check in, smiling at each other in a "What have we let ourselves in for?" way.

"Welcome to the Whisperwood." An older woman with white-blonde hair and lots of blue eye makeup stood behind the desk, looking as if her smile might hide slightly gritted teeth. After checking them in and giving them directions to the kitchen, where she assured them they could leave their boxes for Sunday's tea, she handed Jan a key. "You're in number 26 with Sasha Cook, and you," she said, offering another key to Elaine, "are in 28 with Virginia Willard. Those rooms adjoin, as she requested. My name is Heloise Invers. Just ring this desk if you need anything, and we'll see to it." She held on to the key for a moment as Elaine attempted to remove it from her hand. "I can see you're related to Virginia. You look a lot like her." She leaned forward conspiratorially. "I went to school with all these girls."

Elaine smiled at the characterization of her mother and her classmates as "girls," and the manager released the key. "I'll consider that a compliment. Thank you."

"Elaine! Jan!" A voice behind them prompted the cousins to turn.

FROM THE
GUIDEPOSTS ARCHIVE

This story, by Barbara Billingsley Mohler of Scottsdale, Arizona, originally appeared in *Guideposts*.

Sometimes, as the saying goes, there's the last straw. And then sometimes there's...the last cat! The time of the last cat had come to our household. Our latest house cat, Pajamas, had disappeared, and when it became clear that he'd never return, I said to my two youngest children, "That's it, kids. No replacement. No more cats."

Now, my declaration may have seemed coldhearted, but I felt I had good grounds. Cats had brought me nothing but trials. Judy...Bounce...Little Angel...Quigley...Duffy. I was tired of the whole thing. As a single parent with young children, I had enough to worry about. I didn't need to be dashing to the grocery store for pet food...combing the area at midnight for another wayward tabby. I'd had it. No more cats!

Well, I repeated my declaration until I was nearly blue in the face, and still my Sherman, then ten, and Ginger, seven, wouldn't give up their hopes. A month went by and they never failed to make me aware of whose cats in the area had had kittens. And it appeared that practically every family had kittens to spare.

Finally I came up with one of my bright ideas. "Kids," I said, "let's pray about it and lay a fleece before the Lord." They avidly agreed.

By saying "fleece," I was of course invoking the example of Gideon's fleece, from Judges 6:36–40. In that passage, Gideon asks God, as a sign of assurance, to soak a fleece with dew while the ground all around remains dry. And the Lord did just that. It shames me a little to say so, but I think I was about to make a deliberately outlandish request.

"Lord," I prayed, "the children feel that we should have a cat. I disagree, so we are coming to You for direction. Father, if we are to have a cat, I am asking You to have a kitty walk up our pathway straight to our door. Amen."

"And, Lord," added Ginger, "please make him black." Her addition didn't worry me. By now I was sure my prayer was sufficiently unanswerable.

More than a month went by. No cat. I figured I was in the clear...until the day I walked across the street to visit with a friend. As I rang her doorbell—with my back turned to my own house—I heard hysterically gleeful cries behind me.

"Mom, Mom, Mom! Look, look, look!"

I turned to look back. There, wobbling up my pathway, was a tiny kitty. A black kitty, no less. The Word of God says "faint not." I tried not to. The kids started jumping up and down. "Thank You, Jesus," they cried.

My friend opened her door just as the black kitty walked through my door. "I can't believe this," she laughed, having learned earlier of my ruse. "That's the Lord's Cat."

And so he was...and still is at age eleven. Named "Meow-buddy," he has never run away, never gotten stuck in trees, never clawed my upholstery, and is, most amazingly, agreeable to any and all kinds of cat food. I guess you could call our black cat golden.

A NOTE FROM THE EDITORS

We hope you enjoyed Tearoom Mysteries, published by the Books and Inspirational Media Division of Guideposts, a nonprofit organization that touches millions of lives every day through products and services that inspire, encourage, help you grow in your faith, and celebrate God's love.

Thank you for making a difference with your purchase of this book, which helps fund our many outreach programs to military personnel, prisons, hospitals, nursing homes, and educational institutions.

We also create many useful and uplifting online resources. Visit Guideposts.org to read true stories of hope and inspiration, access OurPrayer network, sign up for free newsletters, download free e-books, join our Facebook community, and follow our stimulating blogs.

To learn about other Guideposts publications, including the best-selling devotional *Daily Guideposts*, go to Guideposts.org/Shop, call (800) 932-2145, or write to Guideposts, PO Box 5815, Harlan, Iowa 51593.

Sign up for the
Guideposts Fiction Newsletter
and stay up-to-date on the books you love!

You'll get sneak peeks of new releases, recommendations from other Guideposts readers, and special offers just for you . . .
and it's FREE!

**Just go to Guideposts.org/Newsletters
today to sign up.**